Tied In Nots

Part of the Rose Prairie Series
Sierra Shipley

Table of Contents

Books By Sierra

The Claiming Her Series

His Temptation
His Disaster
His Reward
His Challenge

The Rose Prairie Series

All Tangled Up
Tied In Nots
It Had To Be You

Interconnected Stand Alone

Yes, Captain
Hey, Neighbor

The Single Dads Club

Loved by the Single Dad
Nanny for the Single Dad
Desired by the Single Dad

Prologue

Candi

"Hey, Candi Girl!" Mom practically shouts into the phone, making me panic reach for the volume of my car stereo to turn it down before she blows out a speaker. Staci Malone doesn't have a quiet bone in her body, and I should've known better than to answer before adjusting the volume.

"Hi, Momma." Turning the dial to an acceptable volume on the stereo, I shift my eyes to the long stretch of country roads leading me to my new destination.

Leaving Liberty College has been a big decision for me, especially being halfway through my junior year, but I felt the need for something different and Rosewood College was the answer. Being on the shyer side, the complete opposite of my mom, the small college in the tiny town of Rose Prairie seemed more my style.

"How's the drive going? Are you keeping an eye out for deer?" It's become an inside joke in our family to tell each other to watch out for deer whenever we drive through back roads. We mean it as a joke, but it's a real warning. Deer are always out and going where they shouldn't during the winter season and seeing that it's January and I *am* on a country road, I do indeed have my eyes out for deer.

"Yes," I chuckle. "So far I've seen a couple in the tree line, but none have made the mad dash out onto the road. The drive isn't too bad either. No traffic and the roads are clear of ice." I'm surprised that there aren't more people on the roads, but with the heavy snowfall in the area a couple of weeks ago, it makes sense that they are still avoiding the roads.

Mom decides to rapidly change the subject, as she normally does. "Good, good. So," she pauses for dramatic effect, "I just got off the phone with Grandma, and guess what?" She practically screams at me, making me reach for the volume once again. "Your cousin Bridget got engaged! Can you believe it?"

Now that all my cousins—all seven of them—are getting older, these "so and so got engaged" phone calls are becoming more frequent. I'm thrilled for them, I really am, but sometimes I would appreciate it if I didn't have to pretend to be so overly excited. Always being the shy and perpetually single girl in the family, a twinge of pain hits me right in the feels when I hear of a new engagement.

"Oh, nice." Trying to sound excited is getting more and more difficult with each phone call like this. "She's been seeing Meg for a couple of years, right?" That manages to get mom talking about all things proposals and weddings and blah, blah, blah.

Once I pull into the parking lot of Stone Hall, my new home for the next year, I'm more emotionally withdrawn than I was thirty minutes ago. Exhaling slowly, I drudge up enough courage to open the door.

Chapter One

Jaxon

"Why do we have to do this?" Pulling my baseball cap off my face, I scowl at the freshman complaining and interrupting my nap.

"Coach said so, that's why," I mumble. "So, stop your whining." The freshman at least has the brains to look contrite as he shuts his mouth. I don't want to be doing this either, but you won't see me complaining, not when Coach specifically told me to keep the guys in line. It's my "captain's duty" as he put it. Placing my cap back over my face, I attempt to relax.

Moving in the new students is a Rosewood tradition. All the sports teams take turns each semester unloading cars to get them settled, and now it's our turn. It's supposed to be this "Welcome to Rosewood, we're happy you're here!" bullshit, but it's really an awkward, "Hi, we're a bunch of strangers who will be touching your stuff and carrying it to your new room. Don't mind us." I didn't like it when I first got here three years ago, and I don't like it today.

"Jax, when can we leave? No one's shown up in an hour." All chances of catching a quick nap after going to Trevor's party off campus last night float away. *Fuck me.* It wasn't like I wanted to carry in other people's shit with a hangover, but here I am.

Sitting up, I glance up at the clock above the entrance to the common room of the dorm. "We have another fifteen minutes. Then you can scamper off to do whatever the hell you want, Sam." A series of groans and thank god's make their rounds through the other players sitting around. We've been at this for three, going on four hours and we're all over it. "Be right back."

Not really needing to take a piss, I head for the bathroom anyway just to get a break from the guys. I'm seriously hung over. Splashing my face with water from the faucet to hopefully make me look less dead on my feet, I examine my reflection. My skin is pinking up from the hot water, but my blue eyes are bloodshot as hell, and I look like shit. Just a few more minutes and then I can crash into the oblivion of sleep.

Pulling the bathroom door open, not bothering to look at where I'm going, someone crashes into me. Out of instinct, my arm wraps around whoever I just ran into in an attempt to steady both of us. All I see is long, brunette hair pulled into a ponytail that smells like some sweet fruit when it smacks me in the face. This girl, whoever she is, is the perfect height, her head nestling against my collarbone as I hold her tight.

"Shit, are you okay? Sorry, I wasn't paying attention." Making sure she's steady, I unwind my arm from around her waist and pull back. She's mousy looking, with small delicate features. She's tall for a girl compared to my six foot one, but nothing else about her stands out. She's just average.

"Sorry, my fault. I have no idea where I'm going." Her cheeks turn bright red as she looks up at me with wide brown eyes.

She's embarrassed.

Smiling politely down at her, I ask, "You new here?" She swallows hard, nodding her head. "In that case, I have some

6

guys here to help you unload your car." Putting my hand on the small of her back, I gently guide her into the common room pointing her to the front desk with the resident advisor who will check her in.

Leaving her to deal with that, I saunter over to the guys, kicking the foot that's in the middle of the walkway. "C'mon guys. The last one of the day just showed up. Let's get this done quickly so we can go." Offering a hand up, the guys stand and stretch as they head for the front door.

We're all waiting on the sidewalk outside of Stone Hall when the mousy girl with good-smelling hair timidly walks down the front steps. She looks casual in her black leggings and a long-oversized hoodie, but she's tense as fuck with her eyes dashing in every direction.

"Um, I'm the dark blue Toyota." Her voice is soft as she points out her vehicle and unlocks it with a click of the fob.

We're not supposed to let the newbies carry any of their stuff inside, so we all pile around the car, grabbing whatever we can carry. We sure as shit want to get this over with.

Mousy grabs her purse and shoulders a backpack as we grab everything else. "I'm in room 205," she announces to the guys already up the front steps with loaded arms.

Shit. Of course, she would live upstairs.

Dragging up what little strength I have left, I carry the two suitcases up the flight of stairs, the other guys trudging behind me to wait at the door for the girl with the keys.

"S'cuse me." The girl squeezes her way through the hallway past the guys carrying her boxes. She looks like she's trying to become as small as possible, her shoulders hunching as she winds her way to the door.

7

The guys do their best to let her through, though admittedly it's pretty difficult when you have ten collegiate baseball players carrying tubs in a narrow hallway.

She manages to get to her door and we awkwardly stand there as she fits the key in the lock and flings the door wide for us to bring stuff in.

It's clear to see that there's already someone living in this room. Bright purple...everything... is covering the occupied bed, desk, and furniture. Pick any random object from this room and you've a one hundred percent chance that that item is purple.

Heading to the undecorated side, I place the cases on the empty bed before leaving the room to make space for the other guys.

"Anything left?" Smacking my palm on Sam's shoulder, the last guy gives me a quick shake of his head.

"Nah, got it all in one trip."

Thank fuck.

Tilting my head towards the full dorm room, I say, "Let the other guys know that they're free to go once they drop her stuff off." Sam nods his head before going into the room to drop off his haul.

I'm out of here.

More guys follow me down the hallway to the stairwell after dropping off their boxes and tubs. Pushing against the door, a high-pitched voice rings out from the other end of the hall, making us all pause and turn to see where the noise came from.

"Thank you!"

TIED IN NOTS

Turning, I see the girl, her long hair dangling over a shoulder with her head sticking out of the doorway. For the love of Christ, I just want to get out of this place.

I offer a quick smile and wave before finally making my exit.

Chapter Two

Candi

So much purple.

The guys who brought in my belongings left in a frenzy and now the purple walls are closing in. The RA at the front desk mentioned that I would have a roommate, but I can't remember her name. I'm lucky I was able to remember my room number after bumping into that guy.

He was just so tall and warm. I swear, I completely lost all capability to form coherent thoughts when he pulled me into him to keep us steady. I'm sure he thought nothing of it though. I tend to go a bit overboard with turning something insignificant into something more. It's a side-effect of all the novels I read—having tiny, insignificant moments and reading into them.

My stuff is everywhere in the room that will be my home for the next five months. As far as dorms go, this one is quite roomy. There's a large window between the two extra-long twin beds, we both have desks and dressers and a small living space right inside the doorway. My new roommate has a small purple loveseat, a cute fuzzy purple rug, and string lights dangling from the ceiling. Hence so much purple.

Surprisingly, we also have our own bathroom off to the side of the living space. Liberty had communal bathrooms for each floor, so I won't miss having to carry all my things with me just to take a shower.

Needing to get started somewhere, I locate my suitcases and start the tedious job of unpacking. Considering I don't have that much stuff, unpacking and organizing go rather quickly. Placing my hair products on the wire rack in the bathroom I hear a gentle squeak of the door being opened.

"Oh my gosh, you're here!" A loud, deafening squeal that rivals my mother is let out by my new roommate who rushes into the bathroom. A ball of energy seems to follow her as she flings herself onto me in a giant hug. "I'm so excited to meet you!"

I don't make it a habit of hugging complete strangers, but seeing as this is the second time I find myself in the embrace of a stranger, I might as well give in. I can't help but laugh at her enthusiasm as I give her a quick hug back before politely extracting myself.

Holding my hand out, I introduce myself. "I'm Candi. I'm guessing you've been expecting me?"

"Oh my gosh, I love your name! Like that Aaron Carter song?" She grasps my hand while she talks a mile a minute. "My name's Polly."

Polly's raven-black hair has streaks of vibrant purple that frame her face and she has the most beautiful smile I've ever seen on a person. Her whole face practically beams joy and with the personality to match. She has incredibly dark brown eyes and sandy brown skin that seems to glow. She's easily one of the prettiest people I've ever met—the complete opposite of me.

Being completely objective, I know I'm no stunner. My hair is a nondescript shade of brown. My face is delicate with large brown eyes and too-large lips that should be seen as conventionally attractive but somehow don't have the same effect as they do on Amanda Seyfried. I've got one lone dimple on my right cheek that throws everything on my face off balance. I'm not too tall and I'm not too skinny. I'm just... *me*. Plain 'ole Candi.

Sure, I think I'm pretty, who wants to travel through their whole life thinking they're not? But it's difficult to think of yourself as pretty to others when a non-existent dating life and no romantic prospects support that fact.

Smiling at Polly and all her energy, I correct her. "Not quite Aaron Carter. Try the song "Sugar, Sugar" by the Archies." Polly tilts her head at me like most people do when I tell them the song that inspired my name. "My grandma listened to old music when my mom was growing up and because of that song, she always wanted a daughter named Candi," I rush.

Polly nods her head as she leaves the bathroom and sits on the purple loveseat. "That's really cool though," she admits. "I don't have a cool story for my name. I think my parents pulled it from some baby name book." We both chuckle awkwardly as I stand in the doorway of the bathroom.

This is what happens when I meet new people. For some reason, I clam up and can't have a normal conversation with someone without loads of awkward silence. Maybe it's the fact that I get too into my own head about things, or perhaps it's the anxiety trickling through my nervous system, but I'm already feeling my cheeks flush pink.

Polly must read my uncomfortable body language and glances around the room. For the most part everything is set up just the way I like it. There's a clear divide between my mismatched nick-knacks and multicolored bedsheets and Polly's purple...everything.

She lets out a playful whistle, "You've gotten everything unpacked already? You must work fast!" Polly shoves herself off the loveseat and prowls through my extensive book collection.

It's my pride and joy. All my favorite stories and characters are displayed in all their glory. Books have been and will always be my constant companions. Them and all the book art and figurines of characters that I've spent way too much money on. But it fills me with such happiness. There's something about getting a bookshelf *just right* that took the longest out of all my unpacking. I almost feel bad for the poor guy who was unlucky enough to grab my book tub.

"Unpacking wasn't too bad. Those guys that helped carry things up cut down on a lot of the time." Sitting on my bed, I watch as Polly pulls one of my favorites off the shelf to read the back. "Do they do that often? Help people unload, I mean."

She snorts, placing the book back in its correct spot. "Oh, yeah. It's a Rosewood tradition. I'm pretty sure that whoever it was that carried your stuff in had no choice in the matter. I'm on the cheerleading squad, and we had to work with the wrestling team in August when all the new freshmen showed up."

"So, it's not from the goodness of their hearts?" I ask facetiously.

TIED IN NOTS

Polly flops down on her bed. "I'm afraid not," she sighs. Leaning on her side, she eyes me. "Ok, Candi, since we're going to be roommates, I need you to understand that you have now earned yourself the role of my best friend." Her face is completely serious. "It's in the roommate agreement that was made when you decided to come to Rosewood. I'm afraid it can't be broken."

Doing my best to keep a straight face, I nod my head in all seriousness. "Absolutely. You can count on me, Polly." We stare across the small walkway between us for half a second before we both burst into laughter.

When I decided to transfer to Rosewood from Liberty, I knew I would be getting a roommate. The past two years at Liberty, I had a small room all to myself and I've gotten used to being alone. Coming into this, I was unsure that living with someone was going to be a good experience, but it seems that Polly is going to make the next five months so much more exciting.

Chapter Three

Jaxon

S hould I really be at a party right now getting drunk off my ass? The correct answer is no, no I should not. Maybe it's not where I should be, but I sure as hell want to be here. Classes start back up tomorrow, we're already back at practice for the season, and all extracurricular activities and partying will be out the door. I'll think of this as my last night of freedom.

Trevor's parties are always legendary. The small town of Rose Prairie doesn't have many things for people my age to do on a quiet night like this, and Trevor's parties have filled that void.

Since Rosewood isn't a large campus, there aren't very many off-campus living options. You're either in the dorms, in on-campus apartments, or you're on your own. No Greek Row here.

Last year, Trevor and a couple of his buddies got together and rented a house just off campus. He's a senior on the wrestling team, and he's been going all out on these parties. I remember him saying something about ending his college career with a bang.

They must have an easy-going landlord because they've done a lot of shit to this house to make it party worthy. The only lighting in the house are those LED stage lights flashing vivid neon colors against the walls. They're programmed to the beat of the music too, so the effect is almost dizzying.

Bodies are everywhere and even though it's January, the doors and windows are open to help cool down the inside of the house. People are dancing to the blaring music, making out in dark corners, and playing drinking games in the kitchen.

Holding my beer over my head, I weave through the tangle of people on the dance floor, heading towards the game room. The dance floor is technically the living room, but Trevor and the guys don't have any furniture in there, instead choosing to keep their couch in the game room.

Only a handful of people are allowed into this room—they're real sticklers for exclusivity. Since I'm not in the mood to dance or hook up with any chicks, I pound my fist against the door until someone gets off their ass to let me in.

After several rounds of knocking my fist against the door, someone finally comes to my aid. "Thank fuck, I've been waiting forever out here." Trevor's roommate and fellow baseball player Gavin stands back just far enough for me to slip past him and into the much quieter room.

"Calm your tits, Jax. It's fucking loud here tonight." Trevor is leaning back in a recliner downing a beer. He likes for his place to be party central, but the dude hates parties. He'd rather hole up in here with his buddies and a beer than be out in the crowd.

Walking over, I give him a quick hand slap before plopping down on the couch and chugging my beer. Trevor's other roommates, Trace and Julian, are playing Xbox sitting in front of the tv on bean bag chairs bickering back and forth.

TIED IN NOTS

"Didn't think you'd be here tonight, Jax. Being the coach's golden boy and all." Gavin sits on the other end of the couch lounging while watching the video game on the screen.

I'd argue with him, but he's right. Coach Hicks does seem to have a hard-on for me. As the first baseman and captain of the Rosewood Thorns or as we lovingly call ourselves, Pricks, Coach has put a lot of responsibility on me to lead by example this season. I don't want to disappoint him or the team, but sometimes a guy has to let loose. There's nothing I take more seriously than baseball, and once the first game of the season hits, I'll be all business once more.

"Shit man," I exhale and lean further back into the couch swallowing another mouthful of beer. "Don't remind me. I'm here to run from my responsibilities, not think about them."

The guys don't bother me as I sit back and drink my beer, simply happy to be out of my dorm room and able to relax. We work to slowly empty the cooler stashed next to the recliner and when I hit the bottom and find no more beers, I head for the door. "Be right back." The guys couldn't give two shits whether I came back or not.

The blaring music blasts into me as I, once again, travel through people to get more beer. Since it's gotten late and classes do start back up tomorrow, it looks like many people cut the night short, most likely due to early morning lectures.

The rounds of beer pong are still going on in the kitchen. Walking into the crowded room I open the fridge and pull out a beer.

"Oh hey, Jax. I wasn't sure if you'd be here tonight." Closing my eyes, I muster the courage to turn around and deal with the girl who's speaking to me.

Clara's a girl who can't take a hint. She was nice, sure, but I don't want to date anyone. My focus is baseball, not blondes who want too much attention. I tried to break it to her easily, but as I said, she can't take a hint. Now, she seems to follow me around wherever I go.

Not wanting to smile at her to avoid giving her the wrong impression, I tilt my cup to her and take a drink. "Yet here I am."

She laughs a little too forcefully. Clara's a pretty girl—a small, bubbly cheerleader—who is used to getting her way apparently. We'd gone out on one date. One that ended after dinner and was never repeated. It's been months and she still pops up everywhere. I must have laid on the charm because now she won't leave me the fuck alone.

"You're so funny, Jax." She steps closer to me, grabbing my arm and pressing her tits against me. Too bad for her, I'm an ass man.

Now that I think about it, it is getting rather late. Downing the rest of my beer, I gently pull my arm from Clara's grip. "It was good seeing you. I'm heading out now." I don't give her time to respond before I'm walking out the door.

Stepping out in the January chill, my body relaxes. No more loud music, clingy girls, or stifling rooms to distract me.

Walking late at night is something I've come to enjoy about living in Rose Prairie. It's such a picturesque quiet town that it's peaceful, not to mention safe, to walk down the middle of the street in the dark of the night. It clears my mind, letting me forget about everything but the sound of the gravel under my feet.

TIED IN NOTS

It's a quick three-minute walk back to campus, but is long enough for me to get into the mindset of school and baseball. I wouldn't be attending any more parties or drinking any more beers this semester. At least until baseball season is over.

Passing the fountain in the middle of campus, a movement catches my eye. There's a girl laying on the swinging bench under the streetlight. She's got a blanket covering herself and a book on her lap and she seems oblivious to me as I get closer to her.

Rosewood is a safe campus, but I wouldn't say it's perfect. She really shouldn't be out here this late all alone.

I'm conflicted.

Common sense is telling me to leave her alone, she's clearly aware of where she is and what time it is. I'd just be the asshole who approached her and harassed her to go back to her dorm. On the other hand, I can't in good conscience leave her out here, especially when I know that lots of drunk guys are going to be walking in this very same direction to go back to their dorms.

Taking a deep breath, I contemplate my options.

Fuck it.

Chapter Four

Candi

Polly has been the breath of fresh air that I've needed. The last several days, she's taken the time to show me around campus to help me acclimate. If it weren't for her, I'd probably have spent the days leading up to class starting curled up on my bed and reading a book. I mean, I have been doing that, but I haven't spent all day doing it. And I say that's growth.

Classes start back up tomorrow, and Polly is out at some party. She'd done her best to try to drag me out of the door, but parties are not my scene. Too many people, too many drinks, too much everything.

Instead, I'm trying and failing to fall asleep. My comforter tangles around my legs as I toss and turn. With a frustrated sigh, I tug my blanket free from bed, throw on some warm clothes, and grab a book from my shelf. Sleeping obviously isn't going to happen tonight, but I also don't want to stay here with all my anxious energy.

Stone Hall's doors slam behind me as I walk down the steps. Where I'm heading, I have no clue, but the cool night air is refreshing. Luckily, there's no one around to see the crazy girl carrying her blanket across campus in the middle of the night.

I've never been around campus at night and it's so serene. There's a light breeze that makes the bare limbs of the trees shake, but I don't find it creepy. It's almost reassuring in a

23

way with their gentle rattle. The streetlights that are barely noticeable during the daylight are evenly spaced all around the grounds, illuminating the dark campus. It makes me feel safe and comfortable, which I know is naive.

The sound of falling water catches my attention, and I know I'm near the fountain. The center of the campus has a large fountain with three tiers that makes me think of the chocolate fountain from my cousin, Julie's wedding. There are these benches that remind me of the porch swing at my grandma's house and I immediately sit down in the closest one.

It's directly under a streetlight, so there's plenty of lighting for me to read my book, and the bench is big enough for two, so I curl up with the blanket draped over my legs.

I think I've just found my new favorite reading spot.

Maybe it's the rushing water, the coaxing swing of the bench, or the dim light, but my eyes start to flutter closed.

The next thing I know, the world is shaking. Shaking and rocking? What the hell?

Peaking an eye open, my entire body jack-knifes up, an unholy scream piercing what was once a peaceful night. All I can see is a stranger's face inches away from mine. I don't think, I just react. Immediately, my hardcover six-hundred-page book goes flying directly into the face of my attacker with a heavy thud.

"Fuck!" Whoever he is, falls flat on his ass, hands cupping his face and I make a run for it.

Jumping off the bench, my legs spring into action—or try to. The blanket that had kept me warm and comfortable enough to fall asleep on a bench in the middle of campus is now working against me. I barely make it half a step before my foot catches on the tangle of blanket pooling on the ground. "Shit!" It's like I'm moving in slow motion as the sidewalk slowly rises to meet my face.

Thankfully, I'm able to get my hands underneath me to stop my face from being destroyed but damn, did it hurt. For a second I'm too stunned to move as I lay face down on the concrete trying to catch my breath and maybe letting out a pained groan or two. With my body down for the count, my brain comes to a moment of clarity. The rational—and awake—part of my brain has finally taken over from my sleep-hazed panic.

Whoever was standing over me was trying to wake me, not scare me. After all, I was sleeping in the middle of a college campus, which admittedly isn't a smart thing to do.

Feet shuffle on the concrete behind me as my would-be attacker pushes himself up off the pavement and comes over to me. "Shit, are you okay?" His arms are spread wide with his palms up in a non-threatening stance. He's breathing hard, which makes sense seeing as he was just pelted in the head with a large book. "I didn't mean to scare you."

Gathering what strength I have left—since adrenaline has consumed most of it—I push myself up off the ground in an unladylike fashion, but I don't care. He's standing several feet away, far enough to not be imposing.

"Are you okay?" He asks again.

Realizing this is the second time he's asked me this question, I figure I should answer. "Yeah, I'm fine." Bending over, I pick up the backstabbing blanket and cuddle it to my chest.

"I'm Jaxon, by the way." He looks familiar, and I realize that he's the guy I ran into when I first got on campus. The *really attractive* guy I ran into. Turning around he bends over, grabbing the book that smacked him in the face, and holds it out to me.

Call me insane, but he's got a great butt. Like, a really nice one.

Not wanting to be rude, I take the book from him. "Thanks." We both just stand there awkwardly looking at one another. "Um, sorry I hit you with the book. I hope it didn't hurt too bad."

"It was effective, that's for sure." He lets out a soft chuckle. "Luckily it hit my forehead. No broken bones."

"I'll keep that in mind and aim lower next time," I mumble. "Um, well..." Turning my body, I toss my thumb over my shoulder, the universal sign for "I'm gonna go."

"Right." He nods his head and shoves his hands in his pockets.

I start to head back to Stone Hall, but I only make it a couple of steps before there's a question gnawing at me. Whipping around, I ask, "Why did you wake me up in the first place?"

He's still standing in the same spot watching me walk away. "I didn't know you were sleeping," he admits. An adorable shy grin sneaks across his face and my hands tighten their grip on my book. He's so cute. He turns and looks behind him, "There's a party just up the street. You're sitting alone in the dark and there are going to be some really drunk guys walking through here." He glances down at his feet before looking back up and straight into my eyes. "I couldn't just leave you there."

Be still my beating heart.

He really didn't mean to scare me, he was just being a good Samaritan. Since Polly's at the party, I knew there was one around here, but I didn't realize it was right down the street. He's right, this is not exactly the best spot for a nap.

"Well, thank you for waking me. I don't think I would have enjoyed that." My face scrunches as all the possibilities of what could have happened pop into my mind. Nodding at him, I turn and start walking in the direction of Stone Hall.

Jaxon's voice calls after me, making me pause. "Wait!" He jogs the short distance between us, and I think I heard him mumble "idiot" before coming to a stop three feet from me. "Can I at least make sure you get back to your dorm?" He must see the confused and apprehensive look on my face because he holds out his hands. "I'll stay at least three feet away from you the whole time." He quickly shrugs his shoulders, almost like a nervous gesture. "It doesn't sit right with me to leave you out here alone. My mom raised me better than that. I promise I'll keep my hands to myself."

And there it is. That heartbreakingly adorable grin has butterflies fluttering in my stomach. And of course, my brain chooses this moment to remember how he held onto me that day in the dorm, how warm and comforting it felt to be in his arms.

Damn it.

I make a show of eying him, when I know good and well that there is no way that I would say no to him. Exhaling a ragged breath, I nod. "Sure. But remember to keep your distance," I rush out, even though all I want is to be next to him in what is sure to be an uncomfortable trip full of silence, seeing as I can't speak to attractive men. Or really men in general.

Jaxon smiles at me. "Understood." He slowly puts his hands into his pocket and shrugs his shoulders.

Clutching my belongings close to my chest, I start walking to my dorm. This time, Jaxon walks with me, keeping at my pace, but observant enough to stay on the other side of the sidewalk.

This isn't the smartest decision I've made, but I could also argue that all my decisions tonight have been pretty dumb, so this might be the dumbest of them all. Allowing a stranger— who woke me up on a bench in the middle of the night— to walk me to my dorm. The place where I live. If anyone else told me about the same situation from their perspective, I would've told them they were crazy.

Jaxon clears his throat next to me, making me glance over at him. He's got long, strong legs and broad shoulders. He's not wearing a baseball cap tonight, and his hair is dark brown, longer on the top, and almost shaved on the sides. His eyes are crystal blue, and he has the prettiest lashes I've ever seen. How is it that guys always seem to have gorgeous, long lashes while girls have to pay for theirs? Completely unfair.

His deep voice pulls me from my ogling. "I'm not sure I caught your name."

"Oh, it's Candi."

"Candi? Well, it's nice to meet you, Candi." I want to say something, but nothing comes to mind, so I give him a tight grin while we walk.

Surprisingly, the walk isn't as cringeworthy as I thought it would be. Yes, we're walking in relative silence, but I'm not feeling weird about it.

"I have to know," Jaxon's deep voice cuts through the night. "Why were you sleeping on that bench?" He's got a slightly teasing tone in his voice, making me smirk over at him.

"I didn't mean to fall asleep," I explain. "That happened by accident." He arches an incredulous brow, making me laugh. "Obviously I came to read." I hold up the book that smacked him in the face giving it a little shake to remind him. "I couldn't sleep, so I grabbed my book and the bench looked like it was the perfect spot. The sleep was by accident."

"Nice," he chuckles. "Is this a habit of yours then? Going out in the middle of the night to read?"

"Do you make a habit of approaching sleeping girls in the middle of the night?" I can feel my cheeks reddening with embarrassment at my quick retort. What's going on with me?

"Touché." He winks at me. Jaxon legitimately just winked at me. "Let's chalk it up to an uncharacteristic moment of chivalry. Won't happen again."

For some reason, I don't believe him. He seems chivalrous enough, so I doubt it's uncharacteristic. I mean, this is only the second interaction I've had with him, but both times he's been helping me in some way.

But I don't say any of that. Instead, I offer him a tight smile.

When we reach the steps of Stone Hall, I stop awkwardly at the bottom. I don't know what to do. *Do I thank him or head inside? Does he want to stay and talk, or go back to his dorm?* See, this is where inexperience sucks ass.

"I'm not sure if I should thank you or not," I admit. He obviously thinks I made a joke because he barks a quick laugh.

He gives me a wave as I start walking up the steps, "Have a nice night, Candi."

"Thanks. You too." But he's already started to walk away and doesn't turn back.

Chapter Five

Jaxon

I knew I'd be tired with everything starting back up this semester, but goddamn am I exhausted.

Coach Hicks has been making us do two-a-day practices, one starting at the ass-crack of dawn and the other after afternoon classes. Between schoolwork and practice, all semblance of social life has vanished. Knowing it was going to happen and living it are two very different things.

"Alright, gather around everyone!" Coach adjusts his ball cap and spits on the ground as the players gather around the pitcher's mound on the practice field. We've been out here since four o'clock and the sun is now beginning to set. At least the weather has warmed up in the last several weeks so we aren't out here freezing our balls off every night. I just hope it means that we won't miss dinner in the cafeteria, even if the food is complete shit.

"Now, gentlemen, listen up. You know that we live and breathe baseball around here. Our first game is next week, and we've been working hard to get into top shape to beat our rivals over at Liberty College." Coach Hicks makes a show of looking all of us dead in the eyes. "But we are also a part of this student body, and we support one another here at Rosewood. That being said, there's going to be a new event that the Student

Activities Committee is setting up and they've asked for our help."

Are you fucking serious? I'm tired of being at the beck and call of whoever puts together these events and then takes it to the coaches, giving us no choice in the matter. They always have to drag us into their shit in order to make anything successful.

"This is non-negotiable. You will be participating." Muffled groans and sharp exhales break out among my teammates. None of us are happy to be doing this, myself included, but I know that Coach has his eyes on me. No matter how hard I want to fight this, I can't let the guys know.

"It seems like it's a Valentine's Date drawing. All of your names will be entered into a bucket, and you will be escorting a lovely Rosewood lady out for Valentine's Day. I don't care if you already have a girlfriend, boyfriend, or whatever type of friend. You're doing this." Coach's tone is clear—there's no getting out of it. "Now go get cleaned up. We're back bright and early tomorrow morning in the weight room."

"Is this for real?" Gavin walks over to the dugout and grabs his bag while I find mine. "What if I don't want to go on a date? Is there no free choice around here?"

I want to agree with him, to bitch and moan about it, but I can't. What is it that he had called me that night at that party? Hazy half-memories float through my head as I try to recall the details of that night. Oh right, Coach's golden boy. "I guess so," I mumble as I shoulder my bag and head for the showers in the locker room. "There's no use in fighting it. Coach seemed pretty adamant about it."

"And what drawing is he talking about anyway? Have you seen anything about it?" We squeeze through the fence opening with our bags on our backs, the sound of our cleats striking the pavement when we hit the sidewalk.

I shake my head. "Nah, I haven't seen anything. I'm guessing that it'll be posted around campus soon though. Valentine's Day is in two weeks, so I'm thinking SAC is getting posters together."

SAC is what we call the Student Activities Committee. They make this big deal about joining during orientation doing their best to rope people in every Fall. They come up with all kinds of different parties and activities for the campus throughout the year. Sometimes they can be fun. I know I enjoyed the Tiki Party Kick-Off at the beginning of the year. Sure, it might have had to do with the girls playing sand volleyball in bikinis, but a good time is a good time.

Sure enough, when I walk through campus to my Business Ethics class in the Beaumont Business Center the next day, there are posters on almost every lamp post and door in sight. They are large red and white posters with an honest-to-God Cupid decked out in wings and a bow and arrow, the words *Cupid's Shuffle* scrawled across the top.

You've got to be fucking kidding me. Stopping in front of the doors, I read the poster.

"Join Cupid's Shuffle! A Valentine's Dating Experience. Enter your name for the drawing to have the perfect date for the big day! To enter, pay $2 to get your name put in the fishbowl. One of Rosewood's Hunks could be on your arm this Valentine's Day!"

Who the hell comes up with this shit?

Chapter Six

Candi

"Ah! Did you see it? Did you see it?" Polly bursts into our dorm room with a red flyer in her hand. "It's happening! I can't believe it!" She's squealing in delight and practically bouncing off the walls. I can even hear her through my headphones that are playing music while I work on my essay for my Creative Writing class. Our prompt is pretty basic, so it left a lot of room for creativity, and I was really getting into it before she interrupted.

Sliding my headphones off of my head, I pause my music and look at my overly excited roommate. "See what?"

She thrusts the flyer into my face. "They used my idea! SAC has started a new event for Valentine's Day, and it's the one I pitched! I mean, I knew that they actually checked their suggestion box in the mail room, but I never in a million years thought that they would pick mine. Oh my gosh, I'm so excited!" Her arms pump excitedly as she does a little dance.

Confused, I look down at the crumpled paper in my hand. "*Cupid's Shuffle*?"

"Isn't that a super cute name? I love a good play on words. My name suggestion had been more generic, but I like this one."

"I'm super excited for you, Polly!" My smile is genuine as I hand her back the paper. She goes to the edge of her desk and drags it along the edge to work out the crinkles, then dramatically takes the tape and sticks it to the wall, making me laugh.

I really couldn't have asked for a better roommate. Sometimes I wonder if we would have become friends if we hadn't roomed together since we're so different. I would like to say that we would, but my social awkwardness makes me think otherwise.

She leans back on her heels, admiring her handiwork. "We are *so* putting our names in for this."

"What?" Unable to control my body, I stand up without even realizing I've done it. "No, *we* are not." I motion between the two of us. "*You* can. But me? Nu-uh, no way."

"Oh, come on, Candi." Polly, the dramatic woman she is, gives me big puppy dog eyes, her pouty lips downturned and her hands clasped together under her chin. "Do it for your best friend Polly?" She blinks her big brown eyes slowly at me, begging me to give in.

"You know I can't do it. You've seen me in action!" Polly had gotten an up close and personal look at just how horrible I am with people. The first time we went to the cafeteria together for dinner, she led us to a table full of people when the table I wanted was tucked in the corner without a soul sitting at it. She was her typical self, chatting with everyone, some she knew and some she didn't. Me? I had clammed up entirely. I barely touched my food, and sat ramrod straight, my face no doubt a shade of beet red. The people were nice and tried to include me in the conversation, but it was like my tongue was made of lead. I sat there quietly panicking.

TIED IN NOTS

She scoffs at me and rolls her eyes, no longer giving me the puppy dog look. "You did fine! That was a table full of people, but this will just be *one* person. Ooh, what if it's Jack? You've met Jack, right? The super-hot Scottish basketball player? He's here on transfer. If you don't know who he is, then I'll be sure to point him out when I see him."

Oh, I've seen him alright. He's in my Creative Writing class and listening to him speak is pure heaven. Not that he's speaking to me, but he's had some great contributions to the class discussion. He's all tall and lean with dark shaggy hair, but it's his voice that has all the girls swooning.

No longer willing to put up with this conversation, I turn back to my desk and sit down in the uncomfortable standard-issue college dorm chair—the ones where if you lean back too far the angled legs will make you feel like you're falling. "You're kidding, right? Jack would be like a worst-case scenario for me. The flyer literally says '*Rosewood Hunk*' and you know good and well that there is no way I can carry out any sort of conversation with anyone who fits that description." As soon as the words leave my mouth, the image of Jaxon pops up.

I'd seen him from a distance around campus since the night he walked me home, but there is no way I'd approach him if I didn't have to. This school is too small to go around without recognizing him or seeing him in passing. He never notices me though.

Story of my life.

That's the problem with being average. Nothing about me stands out.

Whenever I see him, he's carrying his backpack around, or in his baseball gear. I've seen him walking past the cafeteria building while I sat on the stairs outside reading. He had a large bag tossed over his shoulder and the tip of a metal bat sticking out of it. He never told me he played baseball, but even I can connect those dots.

Polly jumps on her bed bouncing slightly as she sits criss crossed while facing me. "No, I'm not kidding. I think this could be really good for you. It would get you out of your shell a bit. You're such an amazing person that everyone should know who you are."

Of course, leave it to Polly to pull on my emotions. Sucking in a breath, I sigh. "You really are the best, you know that?" I turn in my chair and Polly is beaming at me. "But," I exhale, "I don't want to do this *'Cupid's Shuffle'* date. It's not my thing, but you should definitely go for it. Just imagine if *you* get Jack?"

Polly swoons dramatically, fanning her face. "Can't you just see us now?"

And with that, I have artfully dodged a bullet. A dating bullet, but a bullet nonetheless, as Polly starts to imagine all the things that she and Jack would do on their Valentine's date.

THE WHOLE CAMPUS IS buzzing with excitement over this whole *'Cupid's Shuffle'* date thing. I've taken to silently calling it the "Hunger Games of dating." I find it hilarious, but Polly rolls her eyes at me whenever I bring it up. I'm starting to think she's over her dramatics about my non-existent dating life. She'd been shocked to learn that I have never been on a date, haven't had a boyfriend, or even—God forbid—kissed a boy. Her eyes had practically bugged out of her head in shock.

TIED IN NOTS

The week leading up to drawing night, cleverly titled *Shot by Cupid*, has all the girls chatting about who they hope to be paired with. It's all up to fate of course, with both names being drawn live in the Performing Arts Center.

"Wow, this place is packed!" Polly drags me by the arm into the PAC which is bustling with people. For a small campus, when we're all shoved into one space it makes it look like there are thousands of us. "Come on, we've got to get seats close to the stage. There's nothing worse than having to do that horrible run-walk thing when people are waiting on you."

"Geez, woman, I'm coming," I laugh.

People slowly start to sit around us when most of the seats in the back and middle are taken. Slouching down in my chair, I discreetly glance around the room looking for any familiar faces. Well, one face in particular, but that's beside the point.

And there he is.

Honestly, I'm surprised that he's actually here. Granted it's not like there are a ton of things to do in Rose Prairie on a Friday night, but he didn't seem like the type to be involved with this sort of thing.

Of course, he looks as good as ever. He's got on a baseball cap that's pulled low over those stunning blue eyes that I've only seen up close one time. His black shirt is covered by a puffy baseball jacket containing the thorn logo of Rosewood.

Terrified that he will spot me spying on him, I whip my head back towards the stage, because what could be more embarrassing than being caught staring at someone?

A tiny blonde girl walks across the stage and stops in front of the microphone as two giant fish bowls are wheeled out on either side of her. They've gone all out with the decorations;

paper hearts hang from above and a projector displays flashing pictures of happy, lovey-dovey couples holding hands or walking in the park.

Yep, I knew this was coming. That uncomfortable pang of longing to have that type of relationship rips through my heart. *Damn, I really need to pull myself together. This is all getting ridiculous.*

"Hey everyone!" the blonde girl screams into the microphone, her hand pushing up the bridge of her large glasses. "I'm so glad you all came out to support our *Cupid's Shuffle Dating Event*!" People start clapping around us and Polly lets out a loud whoop, her excitement drawing the eyes of everyone in our row.

God kill me now.

Our hostess gives us a moment to calm down before going over the directions. "In case you don't know me, I'm Quinn, the VP of Student Activities. This event was inspired by a suggestion put into our box in the mailroom, so if you have an idea, we'd love to hear it." I look over at Polly, who is sitting on the edge of her seat, bouncing up and down, and give her a playful nudge. "Here's how this is going to work. We will draw two names at a time, one from the guys and one from the ladies," her arms extend to either side showcasing each bowl. "This is how you will be matched with your Valentine's Date! If your name is drawn, please make your way to the stage and stand with your Cupid match."

Let the games begin.

Chapter Seven

Jaxon

Winding through the crowd of students in the PAC, I spot Trevor and Gavin sitting at the back and I grab the empty chair next to them and plop down.

"What's up, guys?" Reaching up, I adjust my ball cap, pulling it lower over my face.

Trevor scoffs. "Same as you dude. You know we had no choice in any of this." He's sagging in his seat with his arms crossed, clearly not wanting to be here. Looks like I'm not the only one.

Gavin nods his head in agreement, his long hair swinging in his face. "But let's look at the bright side, maybe our names won't even be drawn. Aren't they only pulling a certain amount?"

There's been a rumor spreading among the athletes that they are only pulling fifteen to twenty names from each bowl depending on how many girls put their names in. From what I'd heard, the female athletes weren't forced into this whole thing. It's like they knew guys wouldn't be interested in this shit.

"Don't know. I'll buy us all a round of beers at Bottom's Up if we manage to get out of this."

"I like how you think, Jax." Trevor reaches across Gavin and smacks my arm. "Deal."

Settling in, I look around the room right as a blonde girl two rows up begins to wave her arms and call my name. "Jaxon! Is your name in the bowl?" Clara bats her eyelashes and winks over at me. "How funny would it be if our names were pulled together?"

Really fucking funny, I think sarcastically. Giving her a tight smile and a half-hearted thumbs up, she turns around in her seat. Why did I agree to take her out on that date all those months ago?

Thankfully we don't have to wait long before this shit show begins. Quinn walks up to the microphone and kicks everything off. We'd been paired together in a group project our freshman year, and since then we've been friendly acquaintances. Now that I think of it, I'm pretty sure everyone loves Quinn.

With great fanfare, they slowly draw names from the bowls and people make their way up to the stage. For the most part, the girls walk up on stage giddy with excitement, while the guys trudge up the steps straight-faced and somber.

Trevor finds the whole thing fucking funny and is causing a commotion around us with his laughter. Gavin can't help but chuckle right along with him and before long, the two of them make a game out of the whole thing. Even I crack a grin every once in a while.

Another round of names are drawn as Quinn picks a name from the pink-hearted bowl. "Polly Reyes." An ungodly squeal erupts from the front aisle, a small girl jumping up and down in excitement as she runs on stage, bouncing on the balls of her feet.

"Holy shit," Trevor laughs. "I feel sorry for the guy that gets paired with her. Can you imagine?" A round of chuckles breaks out around us.

"And paired with Polly is..." Quinn dramatically swishes her hand through the names, pulling one at random and unfolding it. "Trevor Blake!"

There's no way I can hold in the laughter that bursts from my chest at the sound of his name being blasted through the speakers. Gavin is doubled over in laughter while my head is tossed back as loud cackles break out around me.

Trevor's mouth hangs open but he doesn't move an inch. Eventually, hands from the guys sitting behind us nudge him into action, pushing him out of his seat. We all continue to laugh as he drags his ass down the aisle and up onto the stage to stand next to the girl with purple in her hair.

Four more pairs of names are drawn, all the while Trevor has a glazed-over look on his face, causing us all to cough to cover our chuckles.

"We are down to our final names!" Quinn pushes her glasses back up on her face as she pulls a name. "Our last guy of the evening is," she opens the folded paper and chuckles, "Jaxon Sharp!"

Of. Fucking. Course. Of all the names in the damn bowl, mine just happens to be the last one pulled. I can't catch a fucking break this year. Gritting my teeth, I force myself to walk up to the stage and take my spot at the end of the line.

"Drumroll please!" Quinn is way too good at all this, the whole place suddenly drumming on their knees. "The last lucky lady of the evening is...Candi Malone!"

Candi? That name sounds familiar for some reason.

The purple-haired girl that Trevor is paired with starts jumping up and down, clapping and cheering. "Yes, Candi! Come on up!" She waves her hands at the girl in the crowd who hasn't stood up and moved it to the stage yet. I try to follow where she's waving, but it's hard to see with the stage lights blasting in my face.

Eventually, several girls in the front row crowd around and pull the girl towards the steps. She's got long brown hair and a surge of recognition snaps through my head. She's the girl that threw the book at my face. Her face right now though is white as a sheet, and she looks like she's about to throw up.

Taking pity on her, I meet her at the bottom of the stairs and help her onstage. I can feel her shaking when I place my hand on the small of her back, guiding her to our spot at the end.

Candi swallows hard next to me, her chest heaving, and a light sheen of sweat glistens on her forehead. Placing my hands in my pockets, I lean into her, the sweet smell of her hair filling my nostrils. "Are you okay?"

Panicked brown eyes slide to mine as she quickly shakes her head. All the while, Quinn is in the background thanking everyone for coming and participating in the event.

We're standing close to the black curtains of the stage, far enough away that no one will be paying any attention to us. Sliding my hand out of my pocket, I touch her elbow and gently pull her off the main stage, out of the blinding lights, and into the black quiet of backstage.

Guiding her to a chair I see in the corner by a wall of cables, she sits down, her head immediately falling between her knees.

I awkwardly hover over her, not wanting to upset her with my touch.

A dull hum of voices comes from the audience, and I know that the show is over with people starting to make their way out of the auditorium.

"Oh my gosh. Candi!" The purple-haired girl runs over and drops to her knees in front of Candi, her voice full of concern. "I had no idea that you'd react like this."

She lifts her head, no longer looking sick and pale. "I'm okay." She doesn't sound very convincing, but her eyes are fierce. "I'll be fine. I just wasn't expecting that, is all."

Trevor walks over to me and slaps his hand on my shoulder, temporarily startling me. "What the hell did we get ourselves into?" he whispers.

"Hell, if I know."

The other people who were drawn are starting to come backstage with us, and Candi inhales deeply before standing.

"Okay, everyone," Quinn pips. "Now that you've been matched, you and your partner need to exchange information if you don't already know each other. We've got a list of date ideas that you can choose from if you'd like. The only requirement is that you take a picture for us to upload onto the school website while on your date." Heads nod all around as people break out into chatter.

"So, I guess this is when I ask for your number?" I smile down at Candi at my cheesy line. It's not my best, but I also don't have a choice. If word got back to Coach that I'd bailed on the date, my ass would be on the bench for the rest of the season.

Her eyes widen before she nods and pulls out her phone. "Here you go." She holds it out for me to put my number in and I do the same. She gives me a soft smile before typing in her name and number in my contacts.

"I'll be seeing you soon Candi." She gives me a shy smile and for the first time I notice a dimple on one cheek. It's pretty damn cute.

"I'll be sure to not pelt you in the face next time." That lone dimple gets deeper when she gives me a genuine smile, one that lights up her entire face. How had I ever forgotten this face? "Well, bye Jaxon."

She turns and walks away, her friend laughing at her side. Suddenly, I find myself happy that I was forced into doing this damn thing.

Chapter Eight

Candi

My head is still reeling from shock at what just happened in the PAC. It doesn't take a genius to figure out that Polly took it upon herself to put my name into *Cupid's Shuffle*. Part of me wants to be mad at her, but the other part wants to thank her. Without her, I don't think I'd have spoken to Jaxon again.

In a daze, we walk arm-in-arm across campus and back to our dorm room. Polly is genuinely excited about being picked, but she hardly knows Trevor aside from the parties she goes to are at his house. Me, I stayed silent.

The fact that in a week I will be going on my very first date with a super attractive baseball player with crystal blue eyes has sixteen-year-old me high-fiving myself. Twenty-one-year-old Candi, however, is silently panicking with that information.

How in the world is this going to work? I don't do dates, I don't like meeting new people, in fact, it takes awhile for me to open up to anyone. I guess it's time to stop sheltering myself and start getting out there.

So in preparation for my date with Jaxon this week, I decide to break out of my routine and work in the library on my paper. Packing up my laptop and headphones, I trudge across campus to the library. I've only been here a couple of times and stepping into the deafening silence of Fowler Library is unnerving.

I'm the type of girl who always has music playing in the background, which I blame my music-loving mother for. I got my love of books from my quiet, reserved father, and now that I think of it, I got a lot more than that from him. *Thanks for all the anxiety, Dad.*

My parents got divorced when I was eight, but they are somehow still best friends. Mom is all loud and boisterous while Dad is anxious and reclusive. They could never stay in the same room long enough to enjoy one another without someone getting up to either play music or read. They're just two very different people who were better as friends. Dad bought the house next door, so I grew up with both of my parents whenever I needed them. Nothing changed aside from the fact that in order to peruse the library, I'd have to use the gate in the fence connecting the properties. It's unusual, I know, but my parents getting together in the first place is beyond my comprehension.

The library isn't as busy as I thought it would be. I only had two classes today and both of them are before lunch. I thought the after-lunch study rush would be in full effect, but people must have had other plans.

Scoping around, there's a table tucked in the back corner lit with natural light from the large windows. *Bingo*. I might have come here to get out of my room and into public, but baby steps.

Setting up my workstation, I pull up my Spotify playlist and get to work. I'm almost certain I have one of the most random playlists out there with everything from the classic music of the 60s, 70s, and 80s, all through the 90s and 2000s, to Niki Manaj and of course, the great Taylor Swift. Some of the bands I don't even bother mentioning to people since they've never heard of them.

After a while though, I completely forget that I'm cocooned in the silence of the library and that I am, in fact, in public. My head is bobbing and I'm jamming out in plain view of anyone who stops to look around. Thankfully no sound leaves my moving lips as I mouth the lyrics, but it's not all that mortifying.

What is mortifying is that I don't notice what I'm doing until I catch movement in the corner of my eye, and I see a laughing Jaxon adjusting his backpack on his shoulder. Once again Jaxon has switched on my fight or flight instincts, and in this case, I freeze. My hands on the keyboard stop all motion, my eyes locked on Jaxon, my mouth stuck wide open as Kelly Clarkson belts out "Since U Been Gone" in my headphones.

Jaxon smiles at me, the corner of his eyes crinkling a little as he does. His mouth moves and he points to the seat across from me, but I can't hear him through my headphones and right now, it appears that my muscles are refusing to work. Wide-eyed, I blink slowly at him while my body reboots back to full function.

Finally composed, I rip my headphones off my ears and manage to close my gaping mouth. "Um...?"

Jaxon chuckles at me again before clearing his throat. "I asked if this seat was open?"

"Oh, sure." Sitting up, I adjust my belongings on the table to make sure I'm not taking up too much room.

He sets his bag on the floor and starts placing huge business textbooks on the table along with a notebook and a laptop.

"So," he exhales while dragging out more items from his backpack without looking at me, "Do you perform here often or is this a special occasion? I'd hate to miss the next show."

Can I just die now? Maybe the amount of pure embarrassment flooding my veins painting my face red will end it all for me. Who am I kidding? I've never been that lucky.

Right on cue, heat blooms across my face and I know my blush is in full effect, no doubt stretching down my neck and chest, visible in the black tank top and green jacket I threw on this morning.

"This was a special tour only. I hope you enjoyed it because it won't be happening again." I try to sound confident, but my voice comes out a tad wavery with my humiliation.

A smile pulls at the edge of his mouth as he coyly looks up at me. "That's a shame. I was hoping for an encore performance."

An unflattering puff of air leaves my lips, "I find that hard to believe." Unsure of where this conversation is going, I pull my headphones off my neck, my long hair sliding across my shoulders, and settle them back over my ears. Leaning back into the uncomfortable wooden chair, I try to focus on the paper that I was so caught up in writing five minutes ago.

Thankfully, Jaxon doesn't say anything as he cracks open his book and gets to work. I'm a bit confused as to why he decided to sit with me. Sneaking a peek around the library, many tables are empty, so why did he choose the one with me sitting at it?

TIED IN NOTS

There's no way that I'm turning my music back on, not with my complete inability to realize that I'm in public when doing so, and while he's sitting across from me. Instead, I'm stuck listening to the thoughts that fill my head instead of writing my paper. Thoughts like, *I wonder what Jaxon's working on. Is he still here? Yep, definitely still there. Okay, focus. Focus. Look at his hands... What is it about guys' hands? Crap, did he see me looking?*

My eyes dart between the computer screen and Jaxon, completely unable to focus on one thing or another. Unfortunately, it seems that he has noticed my super discrete observation skills. The corners of his mouth pull up and his shoulders roll while he jots down notes in his notebook. If he can sit here and get his work done, then so can I.

Working out some of the tension that has gathered in my neck, I turn my attention to my computer screen instead of the attractive baseball player sitting across from me. Before long, I'm back in my writing groove, even without music blaring in my ears. Time fades into the background with the clack of each key, the sun slowly making its way across the sky in the window next to me.

"Hey, Candi?" Looking up, Jaxon has started to pack his items back into his bag while I was too engrossed in my writing to notice.

"Yeah?" I ask while sliding my unused headphones off my head.

"I've got to go to practice, but I wanted to let you know about the Valentine's Date before I go." He hoists his bag over his shoulder.

"Um, okay." I'm almost ninety-nine percent certain that he's going to back out of it, so I'm mentally preparing myself for the letdown. I'm disappointed, sure, but also a tad bit relieved. The bright side is that I no longer have to agonize over the possible awkwardness and uncomfortable silence that will most likely be the majority of the date. I highly doubt I'll be able to string enough words together without turning red.

He pushes his chair back to the table, "You live in Stone Hall, right?" I give him a quick nod and he continues. "I'll pick you up at six thirty on Friday. See you then, Candi." With a dazzling smile, he lowers his head and walks away.

My brain is short-circuiting as he walks through the library and out the doors. Wait? This is really happening. Is he for real going to take me on a date? Anxiety rolls through my stomach, coupled with confusing excitement over this turn of events.

Chapter Nine

Jaxon

Anytime I think of Candi, a grin slides across my face. She's always surprising me, whether it's throwing a book in my face, or acting out a full-on concert in the library. Then there was her genuine fear when her name was called for *Cupid's Shuffle*, and the way she always seems to struggle with the right words. I can't wrap my head around her and I want to know more.

Perhaps fate—or cupid himself—knew what they were doing when they decided to put my name with hers.

I'd taken Quinn up on her offer to get a list of ideas for the date and I agree that she had the perfect plan. When I asked her about it, she said, "I figured you'd get your sh—stuff together and come find me eventually," before jotting a list down on post-it and handing it to me.

Sliding my hands in the pockets of my nice jeans, I walk across campus to Stone Hall. I've been dying to have a conversation with her since we worked in the library, but I don't want to push my luck. I get the impression that she's timid and I don't want to overwhelm her. The campus is alive with people getting ready for their dates and SAC is hosting a Romcom Movie Night in the Student Center lounge.

Checking the time on my phone, I'm a few minutes early. I'm now realizing that I don't know which room she's in—I only know she lives in Stone Hall from the vague memory of dropping her off here and her making me laugh at something she'd said. So, I wait. Like an idiot, I pace back and forth at the bottom of the steps leading up to Stone Hall hoping that Candi will show up. Not that she won't show up.

Shit, am I nervous?

It's possible. For the past three years, my life has been school and baseball. Sure, there was that unfortunate lapse in judgment that was Clara—a date that I am hoping she gets over soon. I don't know how much longer I can deal with the clinginess. I've never been one to be on the lookout for girls, I just sit back and wait for them to approach me, and it hasn't failed me yet. Except that Candi isn't the one who has been searching me out. It's the opposite—I'm the one always on the lookout for her.

Wonder what that means...

Shaking off the thought, I type out a text to Trevor who has been complaining all week about his date with "purple-haired Polly" as he calls her. He said he was doing something simple to keep his coach off his back. I'm honestly curious as to what his plans are. As soon as I hit the send button, the door to Stone Hall is pushed open and a group of giggling girls bounces down the steps.

Following just behind them is Candi, her hands twisting and her eyes looking at her feet in a pair of skin-tight dark jeans that immediately grab my attention, black ankle boots, and a flowy red top. She's carrying a jacket in the crook of her arm, and she looks as sweet as her name. That long, sweet-smelling hair is lightly curled and bounces halfway down her back. But it's her face that has my heart-stopping.

Her brown eyes look impossibly bigger with makeup and are framed with long lashes. That plump mouth of hers is glossy and makes me want to feel them against my own.

Holy shit, get it together.

Smiling at her like an idiot, she finally notices me standing at the bottom of the stairs and her steps falter. She doesn't smile, wave, or say anything. She just gets the deepest blush I think I've ever seen on a person, her lips rolling together as she glances away from me.

"Did you forget something?" She still hasn't moved off the step and I'm curious about what is going on in that head of hers. "We can go in and get it if we need to."

Her head tilts to the side, her eyebrows drawing together like she's trying to solve a physics problem. "What?"

"I asked if you forgot something. You stopped so suddenly that I figured you left something behind and needed to go get it." A small chuckle leaves my lips as she finally descends the last few steps of the stairs.

"Oh, no. I didn't forget anything. I was just surprised you're here."

Dramatically, I throw a hand over my heart. "Ouch, thought I'd forget about our date?"

"Actually, yeah," she admits, her voice soft and low.

I wonder what she'd do if she learned that all I've thought about this week is this date.

We turn and start walking into the parking lot and I point out my car to her. Remembering my manners right as she reaches for the passenger side of the car, I sprint over to her side to open the door for her.

Candi stands back and watches me make a fool of myself, a small hum coming from her throat.

"What was that for?"

She slides past me and stands on the other side of the door, not making a move to sit, but instead she's eying me. "What was what for?" A shy grin peeks at the corner of her mouth, letting me know she's in a teasing mood.

"That 'hmm' noise you made." Placing my hands on top of the door frame, I lean into her and her eyes go wide.

"I just thought you said that chivalry wasn't your thing. Yet here you are." With a pointed look, she glances at her open car door and me standing there holding it open for her.

My brain is trying to sift through any conversations I've had with her, but I come up blank. "Don't get too used to it," I tease before giving her a quick wink.

And there's that blush again.

She's silent as we make the short drive from the Rosewood Campus to Rose Prairie town square. The whole town is decked out in hearts with red, pink, and white *everywhere*. The gazebo in the center of the square is decorated with soft pink lights, red roses, large sparkly hearts, and a cupid or two. Speaking of cupid, there's a giant cherub shooting a bow and arrow at a woman in a red dress, both of the faces cut out for a photo opportunity.

This is what listening to Quinn gets me. She had suggested coming to the center of town for the first annual Valentine's Day Love Festival. Something similar takes place on Christmas Eve, but this one is all focused on the day of love.

According to the note Quinn handed me, many of the small businesses located around the town square are offering activities for couples so that they can stay in town and don't have to leave Rose Prairie for a good time.

"Oh wow!" Candi's head swivels as she looks out the window at the spectacle around us. "We *have* to take our picture in the cupid cut out!" She lets out a giggle as I manage to find a parking spot.

"Seriously?"

"Yes! We have to take our pictures anyway for SAC or whatever, right? This will be fun." Her whole face lights up and I don't think I could deny her anything right now.

Reaching for the handle, I open the door. "Alright," I say with a sigh, "c'mon."

Chapter Ten

Candi

To say I'm a complete wreck is an understatement. Polly worked some sort of magic and made me look like I came straight from a set on the CW. She scoured through my closet full of comfy hoodies and sweaters and somehow managed to find tight black jeans with artfully placed distressed areas that I didn't even know I owned, most likely thanks to my mother. Polly then threw a fit when I didn't own any blouses deemed date appropriate and quickly tossed this red one at me and shoved me out the door.

I feel a bit out of place. One, going on a date is a complete anomaly to me. Two, Polly has me in heels, a measly two-inch heel on a boot, but a heel is a heel and my feet are already killing me and we've barely gone anywhere. Three, Jaxon is too gorgeous for words, which is why I've found it almost impossible to speak since he picked me up.

The one thing that has me excited is seeing the giant cut-outs of cupid shooting his arrow. My dorky self is super excited to stick my head through the hole with Jaxon. It also will get the awkward feeling of having to take a picture with your date out of the way for the photo SAC wants. This will be fun and low-pressure which is exactly what I need right now.

Jaxon doesn't open my door for me, but I wasn't expecting him to. I wait for him by the trunk of the car and I get the opportunity to watch him. His hair is styled and not covered by his normal baseball cap, his blue eyes are clear and bright. He's wearing a white button-down and blue jeans, casual but still date appropriate. There never fails to be butterflies in my stomach when I look at him, even more so now since I know that I will be spending the evening with him.

I can see that he really doesn't want to take this picture and that makes me that much more excited to do it. He can tell I'm happy about it, my grin starting to spread across my cheeks, and he rolls his eyes and offers up a hand to walk me across the street.

Panic slides down my spine, my mind once again overthinking. *What if my hands are sweaty? There's no way he will like me if my hands are sweaty. I'm sure it's just a kind gesture, nothing more than another moment of "uncharacteristic chivalry" from him. That's got to be it. There's no way that he would want to hold hands with me. He's just being nice.*

Of course, all of this takes place within the span of a nanosecond, and I carefully place my hand in his. His palm is rough and warm and large. His giant hand seems to swallow mine in his grasp and for once in my life, I feel dainty.

At this moment, I'm not a completely average girl with average features and average *everything*. I'm the girl that is holding Jaxon's hand and it feels like I'm finally *more*. More special, more attractive.

He holds my hand the entire way across the street, carefully maneuvering us between the parked cars lining the sidewalk. Once my foot reaches the cracked pavement, I don't know what to do about my hand still in his. Do I let it go? Does he want to hold my hand?

TIED IN NOTS

What do I do?

Not wanting to be the girl that holds the guy's hands too long and makes it weird, I quickly loosen my grip and slide my hand out of his. Jaxon's fingers flex the slightest bit when he realizes what I've done, but I'm busy walking towards cupid and his lady trying to run from what I just felt.

What is it about Jaxon that makes me feel so...so...unsettled?

Being an introvert with social anxiety, it takes me longer than the average person to warm up to others. Especially when that person is a ridiculously attractive guy whom I'm on a date with, has endured me throwing a book in his face, and witnessed me outwardly enjoying my music in what has to be one of my most embarrassing moments.

There's a small line to get pictures taken, so my 'running' is at an end. Jaxon settles beside me, shaking his head and chuckling as he slides his hands into his pockets. There are couples walking hand in hand around the square, taking pictures in front of the giant glitter hearts, and generally exuding love and romance.

"What is it about this cupid that has you so excited?" Jaxon leans in and nudges my shoulder, drawing my attention back from the wandering crowd to the man standing beside me.

Well, here goes nothing. "I could ask you why you *aren't* excited about this cupid. There's so much potential here." Gesturing to the line before us, which is slowly getting closer and closer to the cupid in question. "It'll be fun." Trying to be as playful as he is, I nudge his shoulder back.

"If this is you admitting that you want to be cupid, I won't stop you. I don't mind being shot by cupid, especially one that looks like you." Those blue eyes of his sparkle down at me, the corner of his mouth pulled up in a smirk.

What. The. Hell.

He's got to be playing with me, right? Once again, a blush creeps down my neck and I'm suddenly sweating. Or at least I feel like I'm sweating with how hot my nerves are making me.

"So you're saying you've always wanted to wear a red dress? I'm happy to be helping this dream of yours come true." I do my best to ignore his gaze, looking anywhere but at his face. *Oh wow, look at that blade of grass stuck to my boot. How interesting.*

Jaxon lets out a deep laugh, one that breaks my concentration on the riveting blade of grass on my boot and draws my eyes back to him. One of his hands is resting on his stomach as he bowls over with laughter. "You're definitely making my dream come true."

With nothing to say to that except to chuckle, I watch him compose himself. Thankfully, it's only another couple of minutes before it's our turn, and Jaxon goes directly to the woman's side, squatting low to fit his head in the slot. I let out a true laugh at that and Jaxon immediately turns to watch me take my place inside cupid's face cut out. I don't have time to overthink every aspect of that interaction because the guy holding Jaxon's phone starts the countdown. "Three, two, one, cheese!"

Once our picture is taken, Jaxon reaches for his phone and leans in close, pulling up the pictures in the phone to show me. I can't help but lean into him in order to see the screen and his cologne hits me, making me momentarily lose all thought at how good he smells.

His thumb slides over the screen to look at all our pictures, and he must spot something he likes because he zooms in closer to our faces. I've got a wide smile on my face looking directly at the camera, but Jaxon is looking up at me. "This one is my favorite. Hands down."

Swallowing hard, I try to come up with something witty to say. "Red is for sure your color. That dress fits you like a glove."

"Nah. I'd say it's Cupid pulling all the attention. He's never looked so good." There's a moment. A moment when our eyes meet, and my breathing slows. We lock eyes, the phone with the picture now a distant memory. If only my brain would stop whirling.

Why is he looking at me like that? Is there something on my face? Oh my god, does he want to kiss me? Do I want to kiss him? What does all this mean? What is happening?

After several tense moments, Jaxon licks his lips and clears his throat before looking out across the square. The sun has started to set and a gorgeous orange and pink glow settles across the sky.

"Here, let's take one more picture." He turns his back on the amazing sunset and motions for me to get closer. Hesitating for a split second, I slide under his arm, my head resting close to his shoulder.

Jaxon leans his head closer to mine and angles the front facing camera so that the sunset is our background. He takes multiple pictures back to back before lowering the camera

"Here," he moves slightly and offers his hand to me once more, "We've got cookie decorating to do."

"What?" Placing my hand in his, he pulls me towards Mama's Cakes, the best bakery in town. Polly brought me here a couple weeks ago for some delicious gooey chocolate chip cookies, and let me just say, they are addictive.

Mama's Cakes is an adorable storefront in the strip of businesses that surround the town square. It looks just like what you'd expect a locally owned, small-town bakery to be. The front bay window displays mouth-watering desserts on colorful cake stands. In honor of Valentine's Day, they have a pink and red theme with paper hearts strung up in the display above the bright pink frosted cupcakes topped with cinnamon hearts. Sure enough, there's a sign in the doorway that says, "Valentine Cookie Decorating Inside."

Jaxon holds the door open for me, his hand falling to the small of my back as he leads me into the cozy bakery. A small crowd has already gathered in the parlor, everyone waiting for the decorating to begin. I'm expecting Jaxon to drop his hand from my back once we're both inside, but he doesn't. His hand lingers, his thumb making small circles that are driving me mad. A shiver makes its way through my body that has nothing to do with the temperature.

"Are you cold?" Jaxon grabs the jacket slung over my elbow and holds it out for me. Not wanting to explain the reasoning behind the shiver, I nod and smile at him as I slip my arms into the sleeves.

An older lady with short white hair raises her arms in front of the crowd. She has a sweet face that makes her seem like the type of person who would sit and listen to your problems while patting on your knee and telling you everything would be alright.

"Good evening, and welcome to Mama's Cakes for the first annual Love Festival. I'm Barbara Clement, owner of Mama's

Cakes and I'll be leading you through the cookie decorating. The stations are located in the back room with all the supplies you'll need. When you're done, don't forget to take a picture for our cookie decorating contest. Have fun!"

We all shuffle through the swinging door and into the back room of Mama's Cakes where Barbara shows us examples of cookie designs and talks us through the methods for using the royal icing. Each design is different: a pair of linked hearts, a set of lips, white hearts with feathered stripes of red and pink, and a cute cupcake complete with a cherry on top.

Ever studious, I watch as Barbara shows us how to outline the designs before flooding the cookie with frosting. When she gets to the feathering portion of the cookies, I practically lean over the table to get a closer look. I have a need to make these the cutest cookies.

Jaxon stands behind me the entire time, not that I turned to check, but I can feel him at my back. I try to not be self-conscious of the fact that my jeans are ridiculously tight and that I'm leaning over a table, giving him a prime view of my ass. But secretly—or not so secretly—I hope that he looks.

We settle into our station wearing cute matching pink polka-dot aprons that make me giggle when Jaxon dramatically throws his hands on his hips and twirls. "Now, I think this beats the red dress for sure."

"Who knew that you'd get a fashion show instead of a date?" He moves closer to me and reaches for the red frosting.

Following his lead, I grab the pink frosting to get started on the linked hearts. It looks like the easiest one to do and the directions are pretty straight forward. "About that. Why'd you decide to do *Cupid's Shuffle* anyway?" He doesn't strike me as the kind of guy who would need to put his name in a jar to go on a date.

He takes a deep breath before answering, his hands stilling around the piping bag. "All of the sports teams had their names thrown in." He's quiet for a moment like he's debating something. "Why'd you put your name in?"

It's a fair question, and one I'm prepared to answer since I asked it first. Might as well be honest about the whole thing. "I didn't." Jaxon looks at me and I drag my focus away from the cookie I'm decorating to look into his eyes. With a sigh, I explain. "Polly put my name in. She's my roommate. It had been her suggestion that started this whole thing and she was really excited. She knows about my..." I pause trying to come up with a way to explain that I'd never been on a date, "dating history, and wanted to set me up. I told her I didn't want to do it, but she put my name in without telling me."

"So that's why you looked sick when they called your name?"

"Yep." Looking down at the cookie, I carefully outline the edges trying my best to keep the frosting from sliding over the side.

"So, aside from throwing books at people and singing in the library, what do you like to do?" He glances over at me while continuing to make a mess of his lip cookie.

"I'm pretty boring actually. Reading is how I like to spend my free time."

"I'd say you are far from boring. No other person has made such an impression on me as you. Except for maybe that book you threw at me. I might have a divot in my forehead for the rest of my life." He gives me a crooked smile, frosting dripping all over the table where it's gone over the edges.

"You're terrible at this," I laugh.

"Hey, don't hate on my lips. They're delicious." His blue eyes sparkle at me playfully.

"I'm sure," I scoff. *Wait, what did I just say? Am I flirting with him? Oh my god, I am, aren't I? Have I been flirting this whole time? Has he been flirting this whole time? Dammit, why do I not know these things?* "So," I stammer, "What do *you* do for fun?"

"Right now, my focus is baseball and school. But I like to go out and occasionally party when I have no other responsibilities. I guess you could say that I'm pretty boring too," he shrugs.

Maybe we have more in common than I thought.

Chapter Eleven

Jaxon

There's one more stop to make after we finish decorating our cookies. Candi, of course, made the best-looking cookies out of the entire group while mine were globs of frosting. I don't care though. Candi has my full attention, and I still feel like I know nothing about her.

I get the feeling that I'm going to have to put in work to get to know her and that when she finally lets me in, it will have all been worth it. She's not the type of girl you date a few times and then leave. No, Candi is the girl that you never stop dating because she's the most special person you've ever met. Even though I barely know her, *that* much I understand.

Across the square under the soft glowing lights strung up for the holiday are booths from local restaurants and businesses selling items. We get food at Eatin' Good, the new deli that recently opened up in town. After paying for our meal, we spot an open picnic table and take a seat.

Candi sits on the bench, already unwrapping her turkey sandwich and drinking her water. Taking the seat across from her, I doctor my ham sandwich with mayo and mustard before taking a bite. Pretty sure I'm going to have to hit up Eatin' Good on a regular basis with how good this sandwich is.

"You're a mustard person, huh?" she asks, after taking a sip of her water.

Shrugging my shoulders at her, I finish chewing before answering. "Who doesn't like mustard?"

"Guilty." She raises her hand, a teasing smile crossing her face, that lone dimple pops up making me want to reach out and stroke her cheek. "I never could eat it. There is one exception and that is with a hot dog as long as it's smothered in ketchup."

"I'll keep that in mind for next time." And I would. So badly I wanted there to be a next time with Candi and like I thought, a blush sneaks across her face. She's been doing it all night, so I must be doing something right.

She takes a deep breath seeming to steady herself before placing her elbows on the top of the table and leaning forward. "So what's your major? I know that you play baseball and that school is important to you, but I don't know your major."

"Business," I say, before taking another bite of my sandwich and swallowing before I continue. "I'm hoping to eventually work for a non-profit. You know, if the whole baseball thing doesn't work out. It'd be nice to go pro, but I've also got to be realistic." I've wanted to go into the Major Leagues for as long as I can remember and getting a full ride to Rosewood College was a bump to my ego. Although it's a small college in a small town, they have one of the most competitive sports programs with a good track record of students playing ball beyond college. "You?"

"English major. But you might have already figured that out, what with the book throwing and paper writing."

"I would have pegged you as a music major with the performance you put on in the library." Candi's mouth pops open in shock that I'd bring it up. It's honestly my favorite thing about her, aside from her ass in those jeans. God was it hard—nearly impossible—to focus on the cookie decorating demonstration with her bending over right in front of me.

"It was one time! I forget where I am *one time* and now you're holding it over my head." She's pretending to be mad, but her tone is teasing and playful.

Finishing my sandwich, I wipe away any remnants of mustard from my mouth. "I'm not saying it's a bad thing. I'm absolutely up for an encore performance, just name the day and time and I'm there."

She smirks at me, trying but failing to hide her laughter. "We'll have to see about that. I don't just perform for anyone, you know." Those big brown eyes sparkle with mischief in the low lighting of the town square.

"I'm making it my life's mission to see you like that again and I don't make new life missions lightly." We're both grinning at each other from across the table and I'm struck by how attractive she is.

Those big brown eyes, those luscious-looking lips, the sweet-smelling long hair, that charming dimple... How this girl is single is beyond me.

Grabbing our trash and tossing it in the nearby trash can, I hold my hand out once again for her. She doesn't hesitate this time, placing her hand in mine. It's thrilling to know that I'm slowly wearing her walls down and that she's opening up to me in her own time.

"Let's get some hot chocolate."

We hit up Tall, Dark, and Coffee's booth for some steaming cups of hot chocolate. Apparently, Candi isn't much of a coffee drinker, preferring the sweet stuff instead of the bitter coffee. Cups in hand, we wander around the square where I slowly pry more information about herself out of her. She's an only child, her parents are divorced but still good friends, and she listens to a wide variety of music.

I really like this girl.

Unfortunately, the night is coming to an end and the booths are starting to pack up around us, so we head back to campus. She's gone all quiet again and I find myself wondering, not for the first time, what is going on in that pretty head of hers. What's going through my mind is how much I don't want this date to end.

Before I know it, we're parked in the lot of Stone Hall. Candi makes a small huffing sound before she unbuckles her seatbelt and steps out of the car. Quickly following after her, I jog to catch up, leading her up the steps with my hand on the small of her back.

"Mind if I walk you to your door?" I'll do anything to make this night longer.

Candi looks at her feet and nods. "Sure."

She leads us through the entryway and towards the stairwell and I'm getting a strange sense of déjà vu as we climb up the stairs to the second floor. She stops at a door halfway down the hall and slowly turns to face me.

"Thanks for taking me out tonight, Jaxon. I had a lot of fun." She shifts her weight between her feet, her hands nervously fidgeting in front of her. With a sigh, she turns and opens her door. "Goodnight."

Then, she closes the door in my face.

Did I do something wrong? What the hell?

I stand there stunned for a moment. This is *not* how I had hoped this night would end. No. There's no way I'm leaving this here. Determined, I raise a fist and knock on the door.

It cracks open, her brown eyes the only visible thing between the small opening. "Can I come in for a second?" I can barely make out a nod before she steps back and allows me inside.

Purple is fucking everywhere, and my guess is that Polly is to blame. Again, I'm hit with a sense that I've been here before, in this room with all this purple.

Candi closes the door and leans her back against it while my eyes scan the room. "Did you need something?" Her voice is small and nervous.

"Yeah, actually. What happened out there?" I point to the hallway beyond her closed door, and she sighs.

"It's embarrassing," she admits.

Stepping closer to her, I put one hand on her waist and the other on her jaw. She looks so small and nervous standing in front of me that I want to comfort her. "I'm sure it's not as bad as you think."

She rolls those brown eyes at me before taking a deep breath. "I've never been kissed before, and you wanted to walk me up to my room and my brain went haywire."

How has this girl never been kissed?

"Candi?" Her eyes slowly move from the floor between us up to mine.

'"Yeah?"

Leaning in for emphasis I ask, "Can I kiss you?" Those luscious lips part the slightest bit and I'm not sure what I'll do if she says no. I'll be devastated to have never tasted those lips.

"Yes." Her voice is breathless, her chest heaving as her breathing grows quicker.

I'm going to make this the best damned first kiss anyone has ever had.

Taking my time, I brush the thumb of my hand on her jaw across her soft lips and I'm rewarded with a shiver that runs through her body. "I've been wanting to do this all night." Her eyes are closed as she takes in the moment, but they snap open at my words.

Slowly, so slowly, I bring my lips to hers. She's shy and timid and *fucking perfect*. Her lips are soft and tender—everything I knew they'd be. It takes a moment for her to respond, but when her lips start to move with mine, I swear I've died and gone to heaven.

Her arms, once tense at her side, wind their way across my shoulders, her body no longer pressing against the door, but against mine. She fits perfectly in my arms and I want more—more dates, more kissing, more of her—but I know it's too soon. So instead of deepening the kiss, I pull back, letting our foreheads rest together as we both catch our breaths.

"That was fucking perfect, Candi. Don't be surprised if I do it again."

Chapter Twelve

Candi

It's been two days since our date, and I haven't been able to stop thinking about Jaxon. Especially the part where he wrapped me in his arms and kissed me. For the first time. I'd be lying if I said that it was a kiss where the world stopped turning because my head was spinning the entire time.

Am I doing this right? What is he thinking? Does he like it? Is this what I'm supposed to do? I'm messing this up, he doesn't like it.

Don't get me wrong, I liked it. A lot. It's just that I couldn't get my brain to shut up long enough to have enjoyed it. But it did make me want more. I look forward to kissing him again as soon as I can.

Jaxon's been gone all weekend on an away baseball game, so I haven't seen him since that night, but he's been texting me all weekend. Sweet things like 'I've been thinking about you' and 'Hope you're not having too much fun without me,' but there's also been ones that make my heart flutter. 'I've been dreaming about those lips of yours' and 'You're as sweet as your name.' Okay, maybe that last one is a bit cheesy, but I can't help the fact that it makes me blush whenever I read it.

Unfortunately, Polly's date with Trevor didn't end as well as mine had.

She'd been fuming when she finally made her way back to our room after having spent the majority of the night walking home. Not only had he been late to pick her up, but Trevor had also decided that Bottom's Up, the local town bar, was the best place to take his date for the evening. The bar was hosting a pool night that Trevor was competing in. He'd gotten drunk and completely abandoned Polly, so she walked her way back to the dorm. When I'd told her that she could have called me she said, "Are you kidding? There was no way I was going to ruin your first date."

After she'd calmed down, she practically begged me to tell her all the details about my date with Jaxon. I'd left out all the anxiety that was constantly swirling around in my stomach, but she loved that we decorated cookies and ate dinner in the square.

What I didn't tell her was that I'd panicked and closed the door in his face, only for him to come back knocking and kissing me speechless. I wanted to keep the whole kissing thing to myself, at least for now. I know that she would want to drag every detail out of me, and I don't want to share that with anyone just yet.

Now, it's a mild Sunday night, so of course, I grab a book and a blanket and walk to my favorite bench on campus. At least this time it's not in the middle of the night. The sun has just started to set, making the fountain light up in its warm glow.

Instead of falling into the story laid out on my lap, my mind is occupied with thoughts of Jaxon. No amount of sighing, readjusting, or repeating the mantra of 'focus' is helping. Just images of Jaxon smiling down at me, the memory of his hand resting on my jaw, the feeling of his breath against my skin. Yeah, there's no way I'm going to get any reading done.

With a defeated sigh, I pull my phone out of my hoodie pocket and pull up my messages with Jaxon. He sent me the pictures we took while out on our date, so of course I immediately made them his contact picture. What I really wanted to do was make the cupid picture my background since it makes me laugh, but a small part of me thinks it's a little premature.

Okay, a big part of me, but that doesn't change the fact that I want to see it whenever I look at my phone.

My fingers slide across the screen as I type out a text to Jaxon to tell him that I'm thinking about him when a loud bell rings out across campus.

One thing I learned about Rosewood College is that it is a fan of traditions, the ringing of the bell being one of them. When a sports team wins while at an away game, the first stop they make once they get back is the bell.

The sound travels across the entire campus, alerting everyone that we've won. Right now, what it's telling me is that Jaxon is back from his trip and hopefully soon I'll be able to see him like I've been longing to.

It's strange to be constantly thinking about someone, especially when I feel like I still barely know him, but I can't stop my mind from envisioning what could be. It makes me feel like a crazy person.

Content with the knowledge that I will be seeing him soon, I slide my phone into my hoodie pocket, message unsent. Settling back into the bench, readjusting my blanket and cracking open my book, I'm no longer distracted by errant thoughts.

I get so engrossed in the story that I don't hear the scuffle of footsteps stopping in front of me. What does alert me to my new companion is a deep chuckle.

I really need to work on being more observant.

"How did I know I'd find you here?" Jaxon stands in front of me, a baseball bag slung over his shoulder looking sleep-rumbled and delicious, his baseball cap on backwards giving me a full view into those beautiful blue eyes.

There's no stopping the smile that takes over my face at the sight of him standing there. "Maybe I'm just predictable."

Jaxon steps forward and sits down on the bench next to my legs that are folded up under the blanket. "I don't know about that. I never seem to know what you're going to do next." His bag hits the concrete with a dull thud.

"Well, I could hit you in the face with my book again. I think that'll keep you on your toes." Jaxon chuckles as his feet push on the pavement, and starts to swing us back and forth. I want so badly to tell him that I was just thinking about him, but I don't want him to think that I'm the type of girl to always be clinging to her boyfriend—not that I've ever had one, but still. I enjoy my space and my alone time too much to overstep whatever boundaries he needs.

"Hmm," he mumbles, his hand playfully scraping along his chin, "It would be a surprise, but I'd prefer something else." The hand closest to me drops to my ankle, his thumb rubbing across the soft flannel surface.

Frozen. I'm completely frozen. Who knew that an innocent touch on the ankle would send me into a spiral? Let's face it, any touch from him would send me into some sort of spiral.

"Um," I swallow, still unable to grasp a single thought tumbling through my brain. "And what would that be?"

He gives me a cocky grin, "I'm sure we could think of something. You could always smack me with a paper. I think I'd prefer that over a book any day." His expression changes from playful to something more serious, his eyes blazing as he looks at me. "There is one thing I'd like to do though."

Is my mouth suddenly dry?

Somehow, I manage to squeak out, "Which is?"

"I wouldn't mind wearing that pink polka dot apron again. As I recall, you said it looked good on me."

That was the *last* thing I expected him to say, and a loud laugh bubbles out of me, making Jaxon laugh right along with me.

The light from the sun has disappeared completely from the horizon and we sit bathed under the lights of the streetlamps laughing while surrounded by the soothing sound of the fountain. Our laughter dies down and for several moments, it's just the two of us enjoying one another's company.

"Can I walk you back to your dorm?" Jaxon breaks the silence, his voice soft and uncertain like he's nervous.

I feel just as nervous as he sounds and I shyly nod my head yes. Jaxon stands and after he lifts the blanket off my lap, offers me his hands to help me avoid the disaster that happened the last time we were here together. I expect him to move away, to reach down and grab his bag, but he doesn't. Jaxon stands in front of me, squeezing my hands in his, and slowly tilts his head down towards mine.

My heart is racing, pounding in my chest, and I think it's about to explode. Except that it doesn't.

Jaxon's lips gently brush against mine in the second kiss I've ever received. It's soft and sweet, and my chest warms at how tender it is. My mind is blessedly silent, and I kiss him back, melting in the warm smell of his skin and the soft caress of his lips.

This kiss? This kiss, I fall into.

My mind is no longer focused on all the things that could go wrong or are going wrong. I'm not focused on whether he likes it, or what he's feeling as his lips brush against mine. No, I'm thinking of how much I enjoy the taste of him, how I've been longing for him since he kissed me on our date. My body is ignited, that part of me I thought was long dead, is suddenly awakened by him.

Losing all sense of time and place, what was once a sweet kiss turns into a scorching need. Without thought, we both press our bodies closer together, my arms wrapping around his waist and pulling him close.

An embarrassing whimper leaves my throat when his hands fist in my hair at the nape of my neck, my mouth opening slightly, and without hesitation, his tongue glides against mine.

Nothing could have prepared me for the sensation that is created by our tongues twining together in a playful dance. I am utterly consumed in him. Seconds melt into eternity in his arms and I can die happy having had this moment.

Just as the thought crosses my mind, the sound of a group of guys' laughter drifts across the fountain as they head across campus, presumably to Ridge Hall—one of the four dorms on campus.

Acting like I've been caught red-handed, I jump away from Jaxon not wanting to be seen making out with him in the middle of campus. Both of us are breathing heavily and he takes his cap off before running his hands through his hair and placing it back on his head.

A blush spreads across my cheeks and I turn my back to them as they cross by the fountain. Ready to escape the embarrassment crawling through me, I scramble to grab my items. Ever observant, Jaxon places his hand on the small of my back and leads me in the opposite direction the guys are walking, taking me back to my dorm like he said he would before we got...distracted.

"Are you okay?" His hand rubs up and down my spine in a gesture of comfort.

Snorting, I admit, "Just embarrassed. I'm sure I'll survive."

"And how do you feel about everything else?" His arm settles across my shoulders, pulling me into his side and I melt into his embrace with a sigh.

"That...was unexpected." There's more that I want to say, but I'm internally cringing, grimacing as I spit out the words. "I'm not sure I ever wanted to come up for air, and probably wouldn't have if those guys hadn't shown up."

His response is immediate and stern. "I'm glad they saw. Now they know not to mess with you because you're my girl."

Why oh why does that possessiveness have me melting inside?

Chapter Thirteen

Jaxon

B aseball practice has been ramping up the closer we get to playing our rivals at Liberty College. Coach is committed to two-a-days for the foreseeable future, and again, I have to grit my teeth. We are all exhausted, but the results of our hard work can't be denied.

So far, we've had an undefeated season. With less than half a season left, we're laser-focused on the championship.

The only thing cutting through my haze of baseball and school is Candi.

We went on our second date last week at Honey's, the fifties-inspired diner that's decorated in bees and honeycombs that I *knew* Candi would love. After dinner, we walked around town and ended up in the gazebo in the center of the town square. There was no big festival or event, but that didn't matter. Just like the bench in the middle of campus in front of the fountain, the town square is our spot.

The more time we spend together, the more I get to know her and all her little quirks. I've also come to learn that when it comes to Candi, I can't keep my hands off of her.

Knowing she's inexperienced, I'm trying to take things slow, but the moment our lips touch, it's like a switch is flipped and there's no denying the electricity between us.

She hasn't talked about it yet, but I suspect I'm the first *anything* for her. Her first date, her first kiss, her first boyfriend. We haven't put a label on it yet, but she's the only person I want—or have ever wanted—this much.

Tonight, Candi's spending time with Polly since I've started to take up most of her free time and they were feeling the need for a 'roommate date'. Whatever that is.

They are heading into Lake Elkins, a town thirty minutes away. It has a movie theater with more comfortable seating and a wider variety of movies to choose from compared to Rose Prairie's dismal two-screen hole in the wall. I guess Polly has been craving Chinese food, and Lake Elkins is the closest place with that as an option.

So, instead of spending my night with Candi, I'm stuck playing video games at Trevor's. It seems like a lifetime ago that I was here, a night that I'll never forget because it brought me her.

"What the fuck, Gavin!" There's no party going on tonight, thankfully, but the way that Julian, Trace, and Gavin are yelling at each other makes me wish there was something to drown them out.

Trevor walks into the game room, hands full of beer, and offers me one. He knows my rule about no drinking during the season, but he offers one anyway.

"Hell no, man. We're midway through the season." Gavin grabs one and pops the tab before leaning back and gulping the entire thing. Part of me wants to call him out on this shit, but it's really none of my business. As long as he doesn't drink before our game in two days, I'll let it slide.

Trevor shrugs, "Thought it was worth a shot. You've gone all dull since you started spending time with that chick."

Gavin lets out a distinguished belch. "Yeah, what's going on with her? All I can think of is how scared she was when we moved her in and during Cupid's Shuffle."

What the hell is he talking about? Moving her in?

"First, her name is Candi." Taking a deep breath, I try to calm down. I don't like that they call her 'that chick' because she's so much more than that. "Second, things are going great. As much as I didn't want to put my name in, I'm glad I was picked."

Julian and Trace start making kissing noises while continuing to play their Xbox. Which I'm glad of because they don't see me coming when I smack the back of their thick skulls.

"Fuck, man!"

"Shit, that fucking hurt, Jax."

Gavin just smirks at his friends' discomfort and uses it to his advantage, making them complain about their game once more.

"I'll tell you what," Trevor leans back against the couch bringing his beer to his lips, "You got the best deal out of that. That Polly chick..." He shakes his head, not bothering to finish his sentence.

"C'mon, how bad could it have been?" I'd known that he didn't want to do the damn thing, but he had no choice, just like me.

"Shit, man. She's something else." He takes another gulp of his beer, draining it of its contents before tossing it on the floor next to him.

Gavin speaks over his shoulder, his eyes never leaving the screen. "Dude, let it go. He's been bitching about it for weeks. The most we ever get is that he can't stand her."

I eye my friend as he shoves himself off the couch and heads toward the kitchen for another beer. We've been friends for three years, and I can tell something's up, but I won't bug him about it anymore.

Eventually, the guys drag me into their video game and the next several hours are full of "fuck you's" as we take turns ruining each other's game. Trevor never joins in, just leans back on the couch and downs beer after beer.

After hours and a couple of pizzas later, I walk back to my dorm room at Thorn Hall. There are four dormitories on campus: Stone Hall, Ridge Hall, Thorn Hall, and Meadow Hall. Each one has a special meaning for Rosewood, and Rose Prairie as a town. I find it all corny, but that's what you get when you choose a small-town college.

As I walk back to my room my fingers fiddle absentmindedly with the phone in my pocket. The urge to speak to Candi is gnawing at me and I give in. Her beautiful smile fills my screen as the phone rings and I'm momentarily stunned by the fact that she's all mine.

"H-hello?" Her voice is scratchy with sleep and I curse myself for walking her up.

"Shit, sorry Sweetness, I didn't mean to wake you up. Go back to bed."

She exhales a breath into the speaker and whispers, "Did you just call me Sweetness?"

I scoff, "I guess I did." Her laugh reaches my ears and tugs on my heart. "Is it bad?" I've wanted to figure out a nickname for her for awhile now and I need to find something that fits.

There's silence at the end of the line, immediately making me regret my choice."Um, let me sleep on it and I'll get back to you."

"Sounds fair." At least it wasn't an outright no.

Candi yawns into the phone, "Is everything okay?"

Shoving my free hand into my pocket, I sigh. "Yeah. I just wanted to hear your voice I guess. How was the roommate date night?"

Bed springs screech and I hear the soft creak of a door closing on the other end of the line. "It was fun. The movie was super cute and the food was good. I think Polly really needed it after what happened on Valentine's Day."

"I'm glad you got to spend time with her." Then something that Gavin said pops into my mind. "Hey, when did we first meet? It was at the bench right?" For some reason, I need to know the answer to this.

She pauses for a moment, "If you want to get technical, then yes, we were first introduced to each other at the bench. But we ran into each other on my first day on campus. My first minutes on campus actually."

My steps falter just as I step into the circular path that holds the fountain. "Wait, we did?"

"You don't remember?" She doesn't sound mad or shocked, it's more like she expected it. She expected that I wouldn't remember.

"Tell me about it." It's more of a demand than a question, but the thought of me not remembering someone who has become so important to me so quickly makes me angry at myself.

"Okay." There's a soft echo of her voice, and I realize she's stepped into her bathroom to keep from waking Polly up. "I had just gotten to campus and was walking through the entryway of Stone Hall. I was distracted and the next thing I knew, I was smack against you and your arms settled around me to keep both of us from falling over. You welcomed me to Rosewood and showed me to the RA station, then you and a bunch of baseball players carried my stuff to my room."

How *the fuck* do I not remember that?

The line is silent while I wrack my brain trying to gain any memory of these first moments together, but I come up empty.

"I take it you still don't remember?"

"It doesn't make sense. I remember having to unload cars that day and being ridiculously hungover. *How do I not remember?*"

"It's okay, Jax." Her voice is sweet and soothing as she tries to comfort me when I should be the one groveling for not remembering the first time I held her in my arms. "What matters is that we did get to know each other. Plus, I like the memory of the bench. It's a great story to tell."

I scowl, angry at myself. "I'm glad you're okay with it, 'cus I'm not."

"Don't be so hard on yourself. The important thing is that we know each other *now*."

My feet move across the pavement without me telling them to move. "Can I come to see you?"

"What? Now?"

"Yeah, now. I'm passing the fountain, and I'll be there in a couple of minutes." I'm practically jogging to Stone Hall. "Just throw on a hoodie and meet me on the steps. Please?"

Candi huffs a laugh, "Alright. I doubt I could stop you at this point anyway. I'll see you in a minute." She hangs up, and I slide my phone back into my pocket and start running. I can't shake the feeling that I need to make this right.

Rounding the building of Stone Hall, Candi is waiting for me, her hair in a bun on the top of her head, stray strands sticking out all over the place. She's wearing adorable bunny slippers with matching bunny print pants, her black hoodie wrapped tight across her as she hugs herself for warmth. She looks sleepy and confused.

"What's going on?"

Without breaking stride or uttering a word, I wrap my arms around her, pulling her close. She hugs me back, her arms clinging to me as she buries her head in my chest. That sweet smell of her hair grounds me and I breathe her in, taking the time to embed it in my memory before I dip her low. Candi lets out a squeal of surprise as my lips find hers. She holds me as tightly as I hold her and kisses me back with such possessiveness that it threatens to cripple me.

I want this girl. No, I *need* this girl.

Our lips don't part until I pull us upright, and as I do she moans her complaint. "Was that better than our first meeting?" I rub my thumb across the lips I'm obsessed with, her brown eyes wide and confused.

"That's why you wanted me to come outside in the middle of the night?"

"Are you saying it wasn't worth it?" I tease.

"No, no it was good. Very good." Her hands rest on my hips and I lean down and kiss her once more.

"Good," I say, my lips brushing against hers. "Because that's how our first meeting should have gone."

Chapter Fourteen

Candi

"Don't have too much fun without me!" Polly prances over, giving me a quick hug before bounding out the door. The cheerleading squad is traveling with the basketball team as they head to a tournament over the weekend, which leaves me with the room all to myself.

Right now, it being Friday afternoon, Jaxon is getting ready to go to his second baseball practice of the day, but later he's coming over to study. I'm an anxious mess, unable to sit still or focus on anything for too long.

Sure, it's just a study date—at least that's what I've been telling myself to keep the panic from setting in. Everything with Jaxon has amplified since that first date, that first kiss. That moment at the bench changed everything for me, all my fear and constant overthinking dissolved when he wrapped me in his arms and kissed me. So much so, that I completely forgot that we were making out in the middle of the campus with people wandering around. I never in my wildest dreams thought that could happen.

It never ceases to amaze me how much time he makes for me. He's devoted to his sport and his academics, but he still manages to make me feel wanted and desired. Last week, when Polly and I had gone out on our roomie date, and he'd called me in the middle of the night just because he wanted to, it melted my heart. Yeah, he'd woken me up, but the sound of his voice was soothing.

The conversation, on the other hand, wasn't.

Learning that Jaxon didn't remember the first time we ran into each other stung, but somehow, I expected it. It makes sense that the super-hot baseball player who didn't want to be there in the first place wouldn't remember a girl like me.

Even the first time we officially met, exchanged names, and interacted for more than a couple of seconds, I could tell it didn't register with him that we knew each other—snippets of conversation that he didn't or couldn't recall. I have to keep telling myself that he remembers me now. Maybe I'm not the girl he remembered at first, but now I'm the girl he wants. At least, I hope so.

Which is why I'm so damn nervous about him coming over.

Over the weeks we've spent together, it's like coals have been stoked in my body, constantly simmering until Jaxon sets them ablaze with his touch. He's awoken something in me that is refusing to fade back into the background.

Readjusting the knick-knacks on my bookshelf for the thousandth time, hyper-focusing on the angle of a figurine, I realize I need to chill out or I will make myself go insane.

Maybe a shower will calm me down.

The warm water cascades down my back as I shave and scrub until my skin is soft and smooth, my hair smelling like strawberries, and my anxiety settled. When I emerge from the shower, I feel like a new woman, one who is ready for whatever the night brings.

By the time Jaxon knocks on my door, I'm much more calm, cool, and collected. Not wanting to put pressure on anything that happens tonight, I went for my normal leggings and hoodie combo since I know Jaxon appreciates me in leggings anyway.

He looks delicious tonight, standing in front of me with a white V-neck t-shirt and gray sweatpants that should be illegal. "Finally," I breathe, wrapping my arms around him and breathing in his warm, clean skin as the door quietly shuts behind him. His hair is still damp from his quick shower after practice leaving him smelling like every woman's fantasy.

Jaxon rests his head on top of mine, lightly pressing a kiss on my head. He inhales deeply, the two of us holding onto one another in contentment. "I missed you, Sweetness." His large hands run up and down my spine, making goosebumps spring up across my skin.

"Hmm," I hum while snuggling closer to the crook of his neck, planting a soft kiss there. "When you say it like that, I don't mind the nickname," I tease, a smile tugging at my mouth. When he'd mentioned it last week, it wasn't my favorite, but right now with me enveloped in his arms, his lips brushing my skin, I don't mind it one bit. In fact, it might be my favorite word right now.

His chest rumbles with quiet laughter. "Are you sure about that Sweetness? 'Cuz I might just be calling you that from now on."

As long as he calls me that while I'm in his arms? Yeah, I'm good with that. Pulling my head back far enough so I can see his face, I nod. "I'm good with it." Offering up my lips, Jaxon meets me halfway. Will I ever get used to kissing him? God, I hope not.

Begrudgingly I pull myself from his arms, letting him step fully into the room. Spinning in a circle I say, "Okay, take your pick. Option number one, comfortable yet cozy purple loveseat." I do my best Vanna White impression, dramatically showcasing the items for his studying use. Jaxon humor's me, crossing his arms and rubbing his chin as if deep in thought. "Option two is the ever-spacious floor, complete with a plush rug for your resting pleasure. Or finally, option three, my desk, the recently cleaned standard issue dorm desk." I offer up my biggest and brightest smile fully in character.

A smile plays at the corners of his mouth as my antics start to get at him, shaking his head and mumbling, "You're such a dork." He continues to stroke his chin while he admires his three studying options. "I pick option number two as long as you take option number one."

"Ooh, I like that option too. Good choice." Jaxon huffs a laugh as he settles himself on the floor, his back resting against the edge of the loveseat as he pulls book after book out of his bag for his classes.

My homework tonight consists of one book that has to be read by the next class on Monday. I grab the copy from my desk, get my comfy blanket and try to lie down on the loveseat. Try being the operative word because my legs are too long for the small couch, so I end up flopping, turning, and contorting my legs to fit on it. Finally comfortable with my position, I open the book and start reading.

"You doin' alright Sweetness? It looked like you were struggling for a minute."

Slowly lowering the book, Jaxon looks over his shoulder at me, his brow arched and his smile wide. My smile matches his and I let out a chuckle. "I think it's a hard-won victory. I'm all set now, thanks."

His shoulders shake with laughter, as he turns back to the books and notes spread out on the floor.

The room grows quiet except for the occasional scrape of pages turning or pens making marks in textbooks. Somewhere along the line, it registers just how easy it all is, that even doing homework together and barely speaking fills my heart with comfort.

After a while, the hand closest to Jaxon drops the pages it's holding and finds the back of his head, my nails lightly grazing along his scalp. I'm not even aware of the fact that my hand has moved or of how long I've been doing it. What draws my attention to it, is the deep sigh Jaxon makes followed by a soft moan of pleasure as his head falls back to rest against the edge of the seat.

My hand freezes on his head, all reading tossed to the side. "Don't stop," he growls up at me. So I focus all my energy on the gentle movements I make across his head. I'm rewarded with another moan as his eyes fall shut, enjoying the simple pleasure of having his head massaged.

I don't think I could stop even if I wanted to. Hearing his sighs and moans has ignited those coals deep in my belly and I can't help but imagine those sounds while he's touching me.

"Thanks, Sweetness," he sighs, before shifting his weight and pushing himself up until he's kneeling at eye level with me. His palm settles against my cheek, his thumb lightly brushing across my skin as he says, "You're amazing," before he leans down and kisses me.

Jaxon kisses me like he'd die if he didn't, and I might die if he stops. I never want the feel of his lips moving against mine to end. The book I was reading forgotten, my hands run across his shoulders to grip the back of his neck as my tongue slips into his mouth. I'm drowning in sensation, heart pounding while Jaxon claims my mouth as his.

We've never gone farther than kissing and short make-out sessions, but this time feels different. Like every kiss, every touch has been building to this and I can't get enough. I want his mouth everywhere.

I want *him* everywhere.

"Jaxon," I gasp between kisses, not able to get out more than his name.

Abruptly, Jaxon pulls back. "Shit, sorry Sweetness." He leans back, his hands running down his face. "I got carried away."

Feeling confused and lonely without him near, I sit up, the book on my lap falling to the floor as I do. "What? What happened?"

His fingers knead the bridge of his nose as he tries to gain his composure, and it's so hard to not look down and see how worked up he is. And boy do I want to look. "Give me a minute," he swallows, "to calm down."

Him calming down is the opposite of what I want to happen. Placing my legs on either side of his torso, my hands pull at his, wanting for him to open his eyes. "Jaxon, look at me." Those crystal blue eyes shoot to mine and I can see the desire in them. "I didn't want you to stop," I whisper. "I wanted you to keep going." God, I can't believe I'm speaking the words out loud for him to hear. The warm sensation of a blush spreads across my cheeks, and my eyes break away from him to look at the floor out of embarrassment.

"Sweetness," his index finger tilts my chin up until I look back at him. His eyes are wide, but tender as he says, "Are you sure? I don't want to pressure you into this. We can stop here; we don't have to do anything more." Without a doubt, I know that if I said that I wanted to stop, he would. He might need a few minutes to calm down, but he would stop. I know that in my heart.

"Jax, I don't want to stop." Gone is the blushing, awkward girl from a moment ago, the voice that comes out of me is strong and sure with no hint of hesitation. "I want you."

The words barely leave my mouth before Jaxon grabs me and pulls me into his chest, his lips finding mine in a searing kiss.

This is happening.

All I know is the sensation he brings and the growing need in my body.

Until the panic sets in.

I thought I had gotten over the overthinking weeks ago, but it comes rushing back, none of it logical. *Polly is going to walk in and see us. No, Polly won't walk in, she's been gone for hours. But someone could walk in. Oh my God, how embarrassing would that be? Is the door even locked? Crap, did we lock the door when he came in here? I don't remember.*

Jaxon must sense the impending doom that's taking place in my mind and pulls back, examining me. "Candi, what is it? Are you alright?"

Pushing myself off the loveseat, I walk over to my bed, flop down on it and drape my arms over my face. I can't believe I'm ruining this before it's even started. "It's stupid," I mumble, completely aware of how dramatic I'm being.

His voice is closer when he speaks. "I bet it's not." When I sit up, Jaxon is standing beside my bed looking down at me. "Tell me what it is."

"It's dumb," I say, because I'm not sure if he's aware of just how stupid it is.

"Try me."

Rolling my eyes, I sit up and point to the door with a sigh. "My brain went to someone walking in the room while we did...things, and then I started to worry that the door was unlocked and that someone would actually walk in. Happy?"

"No," he says over his shoulder walking through the room and over to the door to check the lock. "No, I would not be happy if someone walked in while we were doing *things*," he turns to me with a grin. "Locked. Nothing to worry about." I watch as he saunters back to me, his cock hard in his gray sweatpants making my mouth go dry. He is one hell of a man. Not that I know much about dicks or cocks in general, but I know the man standing in front of me is *big*. Jaxon notices me checking him out and chuckles. "Are you better now?" he asks, teasing.

Biting my lip, I nod at him, and without another word, he stands in front of me and removes his shirt. Did I say my mouth was dry? It's the Sahara Desert now. He's got muscles on top of muscles and I'm speechless. Baseball does a body *well*.

Shirt now in a pile on the floor, he settles himself between my legs that are draped over the edge of the bed, his hand coming around the back of my neck and fisting in my hair. "Don't worry Sweetness, I've got you." His free hand finds the edge of my hoodie and slides under it, his warm palm leaving goosebumps in its wake as he slowly drags it up. His palm hits my rib cage where he hisses. "You're not wearing a bra?"

Jaxon leans down and presses his forehead to mine while the hand under my top moves to cup my small breast, his thumb rubs slowly against my hard nipple, making me suck in a breath. "No," I gasp, "There's no need for one." His thumb doesn't stop circling the bud, making the pounding of my clit even more urgent.

"Shit," he breathes, and without warning the hand fisted in my hair falls to my hoodie as he quickly lifts it over my head. Before I have time to register what's happening, my nipple is firmly in his mouth as he nips at it, making me moan and my back arch.

This, I had never imagined. I never knew that I could be coming undone with his mouth on my breast, but here I am, squirming in his arms as sensation travels through my body and I can feel the wetness between my legs. He feels so *good*.

"Jax," I manage to croak out while he alternates between sucking and nibbling, taking turns with both breasts.

"Lay down," he orders, and I don't hesitate, settling myself in the middle of the bed naked from the waist up and not feeling ashamed. He crawls onto the bed and sits on his knees between my thighs. "I'm going to take these off and then I'm going to lick your pussy Sweetness. I bet you're just as sweet as your name."

Oh. My. God.

I'm going to die and go to heaven.

Jaxon's large hands slide up my thighs until he reaches the band of my leggings and slips his hands inside, gently gliding the fabric off my body until I'm laying naked underneath him. Thank God I shaved.

He tosses my pants to the floor and pauses, smiling down at me. "Ready Sweetness?"

Licking my lips, I mumble, "Mmhmm," and I watch as he lowers himself until he's right in front of my center, his warm breath fanning across my skin. With a wicked grin, he wrenches my legs wider, placing both thighs over his shoulders as he slowly lowers his head and licks.

My body involuntarily jerks as his hot tongue presses against my clit, pure pleasure coursing through me. A pleasure I've never felt before. He tortures me with long, slow licks, making me writhe beneath him. His tongue swirls across my throbbing clit as he sinks one finger into me, making me cry out.

Jaxon pauses, his mouth lifting off of me. "Sweetness, you okay?"

I want to kill him for stopping, but I'm secretly thankful that he's checking on me. "Yeah," I pant, "All good." For emphasis, I even give him a thumbs-up that makes him chuckle before he settles his mouth over me once more.

His tongue and finger move together, and when he adds a second finger, my eyes roll back into my skull. He's scissoring them inside me, stretching me, but also dragging against my sensitive walls making my muscles clench around him. Every move of his fingers and swipe of his tongue is stoking the flames that have engulfed me. The pleasure builds higher before it topples over, my orgasm crashing through me, muscles spasming as he continues to lick and stroke me, dragging out my orgasm for as long as possible.

I'm completely incoherent with all the hormones traveling through my veins. My chest heaves as I try to come back down because I'm certain my soul has left my body. Jaxon kisses up my stomach to my neck, his hands never leaving my body. "Don't move Sweetness, I'll be right back." The bed bounces without his weight on it, but I don't think I'm going to move anytime soon.

When he comes back to the bed, he's completely naked and I'm momentarily stunned by his beauty. The mattress creaks under his weight as he settles back between my thighs leaning back on his knees. "Are you sure?" He asks one more time.

"Yes, Jax," I chuckle, "I'm sure." I've never been more sure of anything than this moment. Bravely reaching down, I take his impressive dick in my palm and lightly squeeze. I've never touched a penis before, so I'm not sure what to do. I don't want to hurt him, but I also want to explore. Breath explodes from him as I move my hand gently up and down his shaft, alternating the pressure of my hand.

"If you don't stop Sweetness, I'm going to come before I'm even inside you." His eyes are burning for me, and I give him one more pull before he rips open the condom and rolls it down his hard length. I'm a panting mess as he lowers himself over me.

I try really hard to relax as he notches himself at my entrance, not yet pushing into me. "You're alright Sweetness," he groans as he leans down and kisses the worry away.

In one smooth motion, he slides into me making me hiss. The feeling of him inside of me is unlike anything I've felt before. A pleasurable and not all uncomfortable feeling of fullness settles through me. Jaxon stills while I gauge what's happening in my body, watching my face for any hints of pain. Sensation overload is the best way to describe it. I feel full and tight, but there's an undercurrent of needing *more*. "Keep going, Jax. I need you to move."

He starts to move; his thrusts slow and smooth. "Damn Sweetness, you feel so good. You're so damn tight. Fuck, you feel amazing." Jaxon whispers praises into my ear as he pushes in and out of my core.

Once again, I'm a torrent of completely new sensations. The pleasure that's building low in my belly is a slow burn compared to the blaze that was his mouth on me. Gradually, Jaxon's movements have me whimpering and my hips moving to meet his thrusts, taking him deeper and deeper each time. "Oh my God, Jaxon. I can't... Jaxon."

Somehow, he understands my pleas. "I got you, Sweetness." One palm glides between our bodies until his finger finds my clit and slowly circles the bundle of nerves as he thrusts into me. That's all it takes before my muscles clench around him, the orgasm making me cry out. Jaxon moans into my neck, his thrusts turning hurried. I feel his cock jerk inside me, moaning my name as he comes.

Chapter Fifteen

Jaxon

To say I'm obsessed with being with my Sweetness would be an understatement. We're cuddled in her bed, her breathing deep and even as she sleeps beside me. She's absolutely amazing. I'm one lucky son of a bitch to have stumbled upon her that night by the fountain. To think I could have gone my whole life without seeing that dimple pop up on her cheek or listening to her excitedly talk about her books leaves a hollow feeling in my chest.

Tonight is possibly the best night of my life and I'm looking forward to repeating it regularly. My hand strokes down her spine, her skin soft and smooth against mine and I sigh in contentment. Did I think I would ever be lying in bed next to a girl and thinking about how I never wanted to leave her side? No, absolutely not.

Yet here I am.

There's never been a girl that could make me laugh as hard as she does, surprises me at every turn, and leaves me with an insatiable need. Candi is my kryptonite.

She shifts next to me snuggling closer. "Jax?" Her voice is husky with sleep and it's adorable. "You awake?" Her eyes don't open, but her hand on my chest gently strokes over my skin.

"Yes, Sweetness, I'm awake." Turning my head, I plant a soft kiss on her forehead and breathe in the smell of her hair.

"Mmm," she moans, sighing as she does. "You're so warm." The feeling of her warm mouth on my skin as she kisses the hollow of my throat makes me pull her closer to me. We're both naked under the sheets, not worried one bit about someone coming in. Letting my hand drift lower down her back and over that fine ass of hers, I give her a gentle squeeze.

"I'd say you're hot too." I'm rewarded with a small chuckle as she snuggles her head into my shoulder. I could get used to all this.

"As much as I'd like to go for round two," she yawns, "I don't think I can at the moment, so behave." She lightly smacks my chest playfully in a warning. Dutifully my palm wanders back up to her waist. "Good boy."

"Only good Sweetness? I thought I did better than that," I tease, a grin breaking across my face.

Feeling her smile against my skin, she huffs a laugh, "You're such a dork."

"Takes one to know one Sweetness." She doesn't respond, content in my arms and slowly drifts back to sleep.

"GATHER AROUND GENTLEMEN!" Coach Hicks aggressively blows his whistle, his arms flailing as he calls everyone to him.

"I'm ready for this shit to be done," Gavin complains next to me as we jog to the pitcher's mound. We're both sweating and panting from the grueling practice coach is once again pushing on us. It's all for a purpose, I know, but I'm worried that we won't be able to take much more of this. Not wanting to share my thoughts on this whole mess, I nod my agreement and we stop with the rest of the team at the mound.

"Now, I know I've been pushing you guys hard this season. You've all risen to the challenge which has led to an undefeated season." Sam, ever enthusiastic, starts whooping and hollering, making the other guys join in, leading to an impromptu mosh pit in the middle of the diamond. Coach stands in the middle, laughing and clapping along in support instead of sporting his natural grimace.

Wanting to be a team player, I clap my hands and pat some of the guys on the shoulders as they jump around. Coach catches my eye and I know that he's watching for my reaction, to see how I lead the team. Sometimes it's annoying to feel like I'm under a microscope, but at the same time, I want Coach to be able to count on me. I enjoy being someone the guys look up to and I'll do whatever I can to make sure that's the case.

After several minutes, Coach's hands raise in the air as he yells, "Alright, alright! Simmer down." The team listens, the cheers and clapping dying off as we all focus our attention back on Coach. "As I was saying," he clears his throat and gives Sam a side eye making us all laugh. "You men have put in exceptional effort this season. We're two days away from playing Liberty College on Saturday, which I know we're going to win." Another round of clapping breaks out. "So, I want you all to take it easy until then. We will still have afternoon practice, but no more six in the morning practices. I want you to rest and recuperate, and be reenergized for Saturday. Hit the showers gentlemen."

Quickly showering off and dressing, I head straight to Candi's dorm room. Since last weekend, I've not wanted to spend any time away from her. We haven't been able to have sex again since Polly is back, but we don't need to. Simply being with her is enough for me. Not that I don't want to bury myself in her every second I'm with her—because I very much do—but I don't want to pressure her into anything.

Stepping into her room, I hurl myself through the air and land with a soft bounce on top of Candi as she lounges in her bed reading a book. My head rests on the softness of her stomach, my arms holding her close to me. "Ah, that's better," I sigh, nuzzling my face into her stomach. She lets out a bark of laughter, her hips bucking as she tries to get away from me.

"Stop!" she squeals, "Stop, that tickles!" I don't stop, of course, I'm enjoying the sound of her laughter too much. "Jax! Stop. Oh my God, I'm going to pee!" She's laughing so hard that it's difficult to make out her words, getting me to laugh right along with her.

"Did you just say you were going to pee?" I chuckle, finally letting up. "Sweetness, you never stop surprising me."

Candi struggles to catch her breath. "Yes, I said I was going to pee if you kept tickling me. It's only natural," she says matter-of-factly. "But thank you for stopping. That would have been embarrassing."

Pushing up on my elbows, I look at her flushed, smiling face, that dimple popping up on her cheek. "Because telling your boyfriend you're going to pee on him isn't?" I ask. I see the moment when she catches my words. We haven't made anything official—I don't feel like we need to—but I think my Sweetness might need it. Those big brown eyes of hers soften at me and they start to fill with unshed tears.

"Boyfriend?" she whispers, a lone tear falling down her cheek that she quickly wipes away.

"Did you doubt me, Sweetness? Of course, I want to be your boyfriend. More importantly, I want everyone to know that *you* are *my* girlfriend. Is that okay with you?" Her chin quivers slightly and she nods her head. She looks so fucking beautiful it hurts.

"Yeah, I'm okay with that. More than okay, actually." She tosses the book on the mattress next to her and leans down planting a kiss on my lips. Always hungry for her touch, I eagerly deepen it as I push myself upright so I can kiss her properly. Her hands grab either side of my face as she slowly lowers herself back down, her head resting on her pillows.

I love how bold she has become. The shy, timid girl who was terrified to kiss me is gone and in her place is a strong, confident woman who knows what she wants. Her tongue slips into my mouth and I stifle a groan when her hips start to rock against my quickly hardening erection. "Fuck, Sweetness. You feel so damn good," I murmur against her lips.

"I'd be worried if I didn't," she quips, her hands traveling down my sides, her fingers hooking in the waist of my jeans. She hums when her fingers start to unbutton my pants and pulls the zipper down before she freezes.

The telltale click of the door is the only warning before Polly strides in speaking as if she was having a conversation with Candi the whole time. "So, I was thinking that on Sat—," she pauses mid-sentences when she sees the two of us in a compromising position on the bed, Candi's hands literally down my pants.

Candi panics, sitting up so quickly that she clashes our heads together, making me fall backward on the mattress, my pants unbuckled around my hips as my hands instinctively cradle my throbbing forehead. Candi lets out a pained groan as she struggles to get out of the bed, her legs unsteady as a newborn foal.

"Oh, hey Polly," she hisses, "I was uh, just, um, looking for something." She mimes looking for the invisible object on the floor, her hand resting on her forehead before bending over and picking up the make-believe item. "Right, here it is."

Polly is standing in the half-open doorway watching the entire scene play out, her face a mixture of confusion and amusement. "I'm surprised you found it on the floor, because last I heard, Jaxon's dick is in his pants." Her head tilts to the side, her tone contemplative, "I thought it'd be bigger than that too."

Too stunned to defend myself, Candi does her best to downplay the situation. She winces, rubbing her hand across her sore head, "I'm not sure what you're talking about."

Polly steps into the room closing the door behind her, before she plops down on the loveseat, clearly enjoying the trainwreck happening right in front of her. "You doing alright there Jaxon? You look a little out of it," Polly's voice is teasing, a smile threatening to break out on her face.

Heaving myself up still clutching my pounding head, I groan. "I'm all good, Polly. I'd be better if you hadn't walked in, I can guarantee that."

Candi sits next to me on the bed, both of us nursing our wounds as Polly throws her head back, laughing at our predicament. "I'm sure you would!" She howls, hand smacking against the plush cushions as she laughs. "I'm so proud of you, Candi. Well done!"

Eventually, Polly stops laughing and lets us tend to our wounds as she sits on the loveseat and works on some homework with headphones in.

"I'm so sorry, Jax," Candi whispers as she lays her head on my shoulder. We're sitting on her bed, our backs resting against the wall, feet dangling over the edge. We're both sporting small bruises on our foreheads, but other than that we're fine. Linking our hands together, my head falls back against the wall with a dull thud. "I panicked like I always do. Are you sure you're okay? I can get some ice from the cafe if you need it."

She feels terrible about what happened, but aside from a little tenderness, I think I'll survive. "I'm all good, Sweetness. I'm fine, I promise." Turning, I kiss the top of her head. "How are you though? That was one helluva hit."

She snorts, "The only thing that hurts is the fact that I pegged you in the face. Again! You might have to leave me for your safety, who knows what I'm going to hit you with next." She's trying to lighten the mood, but I can sense the emotions underneath.

Lifting her head with my hand, I look down at the girl who has caught all my attention, stroking the cheek that hides the dimple I love so much. "Sweetness, you're going to have to do better than that to get me to leave." Gently I bring my mouth to hers and kiss her soft lips. "Plus," I smile, "I'm interested to see what you manage to throw at me next."

Chapter Sixteen

Candi

The baseball stadium is packed as students and faculty from both schools file into the seating area. Haverford Baseball Field isn't large by any means, but it's a good size for a small-town college baseball field. The rose-red stadium chairs are jam-packed with people taking their seats as the players warm up on the field. I've already spotted Jaxon warming up at first base, and let me just say, God bless the man that created baseball pants.

Polly and I link arms as we push our way through the gathering crowd, heading toward a section marked off for Rosewood students. Her cheerleader friends are already there and are saving us some seats. The sun is blazing overhead and I'm thankful my boyfriend lent me one of his ballcaps.

It still feels so surreal that I, Candi Malone, perpetually single and awkward twenty-one-year-old have a super-hot baseball-playing boyfriend. I blush just thinking about it.

There had been an underlying feeling that leaving Liberty College for Rosewood was the best decision for me, and I'm beginning to think that Jaxon is the reason.

"Oh, there they are!" Polly points to the front row of the student section full of stunning cheerleaders with their flawless makeup and the emblem of Rosewood painted on their cheeks. Polly was invited to get ready for the game with them but decided to stick with me, so she missed out on the face paint. "Hey, girls!" She shouts as we reach the row where they've saved two seats in the middle of the aisle for us.

It's so close to the field that I could shout at Jaxon and he'd hear me. I want to, but I don't, knowing that this game is important to him. We'd parted last night with a quick kiss at the bottom of Stone Hall's front steps, his shoulders tense with the coming game.

Taking our seats, I get myself situated while music plays through the speakers. Maybe I should send them a mix of better songs, these are severely lacking.

"Hi," a perky voice chirps next to me. A small, beautiful blonde cheerleader holds her hand out to me. "I'm Clara. I don't think we've met yet. Aren't you Polly's roommate?"

Her big blue eyes bat at me while I shake her hand. "Yeah. Hi, I'm Candi." Her lipstick-painted mouth pops open at the mention of my name.

"Oh my God, your name is Candi? How sweet!" Her blazing white teeth sparkle in the sunlight, and I feel myself shrink next to her. Am I going to have to deal with this the whole game? Polly is talking to the girl next to her and isn't paying any attention to me, which is fine, but that means I have no one to rescue me.

Before Clara can drag me further into an unwanted conversation, the announcer comes over the speaker with all of the opening game procedures. Then, the players are individually announced, and I find myself nervous for Jaxon as his name is called. "First baseman, Jaxon Sharp!" Jaxon steps forward and waves a gloved hand toward the crowd and I'm beaming at him clapping my hands in support. But Clara?

Clara jumps out of her seat and screams at the top of her lungs, her arms thrown in the air as she cheers.

Girl, what the fuck?

I've never met this girl, and Jaxon's never mentioned her, so what the hell is going on? Thinking back through the past month with Jaxon not once has he brought up anything other than baseball, school, and his mom.

He's spoken about his home life in bits and pieces. He was raised by a single mom who struggled when he was younger. She's the reason he wants to work in a non-profit once he graduates. They're pretty close and he calls her once a week just to check on her. I briefly met some of his friends, Trevor and Gavin mainly with a couple of baseball players thrown in, but no Clara. No girls ever.

Do they have a history together? Why has he never mentioned her? Is he keeping her a secret? But why would he do that? We've been together basically nonstop since Valentine's Day, he couldn't possibly have had time to see me and this chick. Maybe I'm reading too much into it. Definitely reading too much into it. Just relax and enjoy watching your boyfriend play the sport he loves.

I'll admit that I know very little about baseball. I understand the basics—hit the ball, run the bases, get the runners out, rinse and repeat.

Polly helps to get me out of my funk brought on by overthinking Clara's reaction to my boyfriend. When someone in the stand starts the wave, Polly drags me up out of my seat, making me join in. She leaves for a bit in the third inning and brings back hotdogs saying, "Everyone knows you have to enjoy a hotdog while watching a baseball game. It's in the rule book somewhere."

Watching Jaxon, I'm amazed at how good he is. He's so quick to catch the ball for an out and immediately rears his arm back and lobs the ball across the field, making a double play. It's clear that he's an important part of the team and it makes my heart fill with pride. Adjusting his hat on my head, I smile and clap with the crowd as the teams switch the field.

"You see the first baseman?" Clara leans over and points to Jaxon as he walks into the dugout.

"You mean number seventeen? Jaxon Sharp?" I ask, playing dumb. "I might know him."

Clara's blue eyes widen when I say I know him. "You do? Isn't he just a dreamboat?" She reaches out and lightly touches my arm as she swoons over him. "We went out a while back, and let me tell you," she leans in closer and crooks her finger at me, "he's as dreamy as he looks." Clara dramatically fans herself and blows out a breath through her pursed lips. "He's going to be mine one of these days." The determined look on her face says that she's not going to stop until she gets what she wants, and what she wants is *my* boyfriend.

Taking a minute while Sweet Caroline plays through the speakers as the players get warmed up for the next inning, I look over at Clara as she talks to the girl on the other side of her. She's a petite, perky, busty blonde cheerleader. She's everything I'm not.

Since Jaxon stumbled into my life, I haven't been as self-conscious. He's never made me feel anything other than pretty and desired whenever he's around me. I don't worry about what I look like at all when I'm with him.

So why am I letting Clara wiggle her way into my head?

For the rest of the game, I'm distracted by my thoughts. I'm watching the game, but my mind is overthinking, leaving me in no mood to deal with the people around me.

When the ninth inning comes to an end, the entire student section loses their minds. Rosewood College beats Liberty College seven runs to five. We're all jumping and screaming for our team, and I'm so proud of Jaxon.

The team gathers in the middle of the field surrounding their coach as he talks to them. I can't hear what he's saying but the guys are circled around him, arms tossed over the shoulders of their neighbors with smiles on their faces. They've worked so hard for this. All at once, the guys lower their arms and clap, running over to the stands to wave at their fans. I catch Jaxon's eye as they head to the student section and a heart-stopping grin spreads across his face, his pace picking up to a run in my direction.

The only thing separating the stadium seats from the diamond is a four-foot-high concrete wall. Jaxon runs right to me, flipping his hat backward the closer he gets to me. When he's right in front of me, he slips my borrowed baseball cap off my head, wraps his arms around my waist, and kisses me right in front of everyone.

Some shocked gasps and catcalls are being made by the students behind me, but I'm too wrapped up in Jaxon to care. I'm left breathless when he finally releases me and playfully places his hat back on my head before running back with his teammates.

"Damn girl," Polly claps, "That was hot."

My hands flap in front of my face as I try to cool my overheated skin and to get the blush to die down. "You're telling me." Smiling at my friend, I bend down to pick up my bag and when I stand up, Clara is staring at me, her eyebrows furrowed.

I get it. I'm trying to figure out why he's with me too.

Chapter Seventeen

Jaxon

With the win over Liberty College comes an enormous sense of relief. They are our rivals for a reason. Not only are they our neighboring college, but they are the most competitive team in our league. This means that the rest of the season—all three games—should be a breeze. Not that we are going to let up on our drive, that would mean throwing out all our hard work, but we can at least relax in the knowledge that we beat the hardest team.

I'm on cloud nine as the players wave thanks to the fans and head back to the dugout to grab my bag. I just played the best game in my college career and my Sweetness was waiting for me in the stands. Nothing can shake this high.

An arm jostles me as it's tossed around my shoulders, "Fuck, man! We did it!" Gavin yells into my ear, his voice hoarse with overuse. Gavin played a great game tonight and his hit in the seventh inning helped us win the game.

Grinning up at him, I smack his shoulder. "Fuck yeah, we did. How are you going to celebrate?" I already know what I would be doing.

"Trevor's throwing a party at the house. Word's already getting out and tonight is going to be lit. You gonna come?" He tosses his bag over his shoulder and sneaks a peek over at me. "Let me guess," he shakes his head, "You've got a girl to see?"

"She's not just a girl, Gavin," I chastise, grabbing my items without looking back at him. "Don't do anything stupid!" I shout over my shoulder as I bound up the stairs of the dugout ready to get to my girl.

Weaving through the crowds still hanging out in the parking lot is no easy task. Everyone wants me to stop while they mention how great of a game we played tonight and how excited they are that we beat the shit out of Liberty. I'm excited too, but my celebration comes in the form of a tall, gorgeous brunette who tastes like sugar.

Sliding into the driver's seat of my car, I pull out my cell phone and hit the speed dial for my mom. She lives two states away and can't always get away from work and make the hours-long trip to my games, but I know she watches the live stream for every home game.

The phone rings through the speaker several times before she answers, her loud cheers punctuating the silence. "Baby boy! You did *so* well tonight. I can't believe I missed being at this game." Her voice fills with regret at not making the journey here. It's one of the downsides to choosing Rosewood, but she damn near forced me to go with the full-ride scholarship Coach offered.

"Thanks, Mom. But don't feel bad that you weren't here, you were able to watch it anyway."

"I know," she admits, "but I still would have liked to have seen that double play in person. How in the world do you throw the ball that fast? It never ceases to amaze me how you do that."

Growing up, Mom did her best to get me to all the practices between her busy work schedules. It wasn't until I was in middle school that she was able to stop waitressing and work one job at our local Family and Youth Services as a receptionist. Even then, she wasn't able to pay for private practices, so I made sure to work my ass off whenever I could.

Cracking a smile at our running joke, I say, "It's all in the wrist, Ma." Her bright laughter mixes with mine as we continue to talk about the game and how practices are going. We talk weekly, so there isn't all that much to catch up on, and we end the call several minutes later.

Finally turning the key in the ignition, I drive through town and back to campus. I have to stop at my room before heading to see Candi, but I can shower quickly. There's nothing I want to do more than spend time with her.

Breaking the record for the fastest shower, I quickly leave Thorn Hall and take the shortcut through campus to Candi's dorm. When I reach the steps of Stone Hall, a large group of girls is walking down the steps all dressed up, no doubt heading to Trevor's for the party.

"Oh, there he is!" A high-pitched voice drawls, and I can't control the cringe that crosses my face when Clara's arm loops through mine, making me stop just inches away from the door. "Jaxon, you played ah-mazing tonight. Aren't you going to come and celebrate with us?" She bats those too-big eyelashes at me, making me huff a breath in frustration. Will this girl never get over me?

"No, Clara, I'm not." I'm proud that my voice isn't full of disdain as I work to free my arm from her grasp. "I've got somewhere better to be."

She only grips me tighter and leans in close, whispering, "If you come with us, I can make it worth your while." Her voice drops low in an attempt to be seductive, but it's no use. The time of being polite has passed.

Wrenching my arm free, I look her dead in the eyes and rip off the band-aid. "Clara, I have a girlfriend—one I'm completely loyal to. I've tried to be nice, but you need to stop with these advances. I'm not interested in dating you, going to parties with you, or doing whatever it is you just offered me. I'm sure you'll find someone who feels for you the same way I do about Candi, but you're not the girl for me." Her blue eyes widen in shock, but I don't wait for her to respond before pulling the door open and jogging up the stairs to see my Sweetness.

By the time I reach her door, I'm near breathless from taking the steps two at a time. Their door is usually unlocked, but with recent events, I take a moment to knock and wait for a response before entering. Except there isn't one. Knocking again, I wait, but yet again no one answers. That's strange.

Creaking open the door, Polly and Candi's room is pitch black except for the string lights blinking on Polly's wall. She would have told me if she wasn't going to be here, right?

Pulling out my phone, I send Candi a text and stand in the doorway waiting for her to reply. When I hear the faint buzz coming from her desk, I know that she left her phone here. Where would she have gone?

A smile crosses my face. I know my girl.

Sure enough, my Sweetness is sitting at our bench—the one that will forever belong to us—her hair dangling over the armrest as she lays there, the bench lightly swinging back and forth. "There you are, Sweetness. I thought you were in your room." Rounding the bench under the dim lamps I can see her red-rimmed eyes as she wipes away the tears that are streaming down her cheeks.

She sits up quickly, startled by my sudden appearance. "Sorry," she sniffles, the blanket covering her legs dangling on the ground from her movements. "I just...needed to think."

The bench is still warm from her legs when I sit. My mind immediately goes on high alert when she says those five words. Whatever is on my girl's mind has me worried. Candi is not one to cry, at least I've only seen a tear one time, but I get the sense that she doesn't cry if she can help it. My arm settles across her shoulders, pulling her closer and offering her my warmth. "Sweetness, what's wrong?"

Candi heaves a large, shaky breath, her knees pulling up to her chest as she wraps her arms around them. "Me," she releases with a sigh.

Who the fuck made her feel this way?

My free hand cups her face, pulling her gaze toward me. "Sweetness, tell me what you're thinking because right now I'm thinking that I'll hurt whoever made you feel this way," my voice is soft but laced with the promise that I would follow through with my threat. Her brown eyes overflow with tears making my heart ache.

"I'm the problem," she scoffs, "I'm not good enough for you." Candi turns her head away from me, her arms gesturing down her body. "Look at me!"

"Sweetness, I *am* looking at you and there's *nothing* I see that I don't like.

"Oh right, like you wouldn't rather have a tiny, busty, blonde, peppy cheerleader who isn't riddled with anxiety, and doesn't headbutt you when someone walks through the door.

I'm just not that girl, Jaxon. I'm not the one that's going to cheer the loudest or wear the most makeup. I'm not the girl with the perfect figure who likes to party. I'm not the girl you should be with."

Every word that leaves her beautiful mouth is a dagger to my heart. It also angers me that this is the way she sees herself.

"Then who gets to choose that? Because I can tell you, Sweetness, that the only girl I *need* is the one sitting right here." At my words, her wide, teary eyes finally meet mine. My hand once again reaches for her cheek, cupping it while I beg with all my might for her to listen to my words. "I need the girl that makes me laugh without even trying. I need the girl that keeps me on my toes even when I think I know what to expect. I need the girl that prefers lying in bed with a good book instead of partying the night away. I need the girl who has the best ass I've ever seen. I need *you*, Sweetness. Don't you see that?"

Tears fall freely down her cheeks, and I wipe them away with the pad of my thumb. "I just don't get it. Why don't you want those other girls?"

"Because they're not you," I reply with no hesitation. "They're not you, Sweetness."

Candi swallows hard. "You want me?"

It's so tempting to grab her shoulders to shake some sense into her, but I don't. "Fuck yes, I want you. I want you more than I've ever wanted anything."

"Even more than baseball?" The corners of her mouth twitch as she holds back a smile. *There's my girl.*

"Yes, more than baseball." I want this girl more than anything in my whole life. If that meant spending every day telling her how amazing, talented, smart, and sexy she is, then

I'll fucking do it. Candi smiles at that, some of her worry around her eyes melting away. "Now, can you stop telling me who I'm supposed to love?"

"Love?" Her eyes widen at my admission, but she nods her head, "I guess I can do that."

"Good. And yes, love. I love you Sweetness.

Before she has one more moment to doubt herself, I pull her lips to mine and she tenderly kisses me back, her fears seeming to melt away with my touch. More than a month has passed since that fateful night when I stumbled upon a girl sleeping on a bench, the night when I found the most amazing person I've ever met. Candi is everything I didn't know I needed or wanted.

Thank God for that stupid *Cupid's Shuffle* for making me see her.

Epilogue

Candi

Three Years Later

The radio blasts an eclectic list of songs as Jaxon and I make the long drive to Rose Prairie from the city. Rosewood takes on its Liberty College rivals this weekend and there is no way we are going to miss it.

"What the hell is this song?" Jaxon glances over at me, a bewildered look on his face. He looks handsome as ever as he maneuvers the country roads, his baseball cap turned backward threatening to make me drool. His aviator sunglasses hide those crystal blue eyes, but I can sense his confusion.

"Oh, come on. You know who this is! I swear we've listened to it before." Jaxon has a very limited range of music tastes, which is why I always get to pick out the songs.

His eyebrows raise slightly over the rim of his glasses as he looks sideways at me. "I shit you not, I've never heard this song in my life." He's being completely serious too. He honestly thinks he's never heard it before.

"It's the Gorillaz," shaking my head at him, I show him the screen of my phone.

"Never heard of 'em."

"After three years together, I would've thought I'd have broadened your taste, but no," I mumble to myself.

After graduation, Jaxon was 'called up' as they say in baseball to a farm team to play minor league ball. After some talking, he decided to give it a shot. I know that his heart is in non-profit work, but he can do both. It's been two years of hard work, but last week he got the call. *The call*. He's going to the Major Leagues, and I couldn't be prouder.

We moved to the city together where I was able to get a job as a copy editor at a small publishing house. I like it, but I much prefer to read my books at home.

Coming back to visit Rosewood is one of our last trips before Jaxon heads to the Major League, so it's a bit bittersweet. We won't get another trip like this anytime soon, at least until the season is over.

Before long, Rose Prairie trickles by through my window, and an overwhelming sense of nostalgia slams through me. I've missed this place. For over a year, this small town was my home. It's the town where I fell in love. It's where I had my first date. *I love this place*. A tear threatens to fall, but I quickly wipe it away before Jaxon notices.

The turn for Haverford Baseball Field comes into view, but Jaxon drives right past it. "Um, I think you forgot your way around town, Jax. The turn for the field is back there."

Jaxon shifts slightly in his seat clearing his throat. "Yeah, I know. There's just a stop I want to make first."

"Um, okay." He turns onto Main Street and I'm hit with a million little memories as we pass through the town square. Our first Christmas Spectacular together, our anniversary date to Mama's Cakes, the coffee shop and bookstore that he let me have a shopping spree in on my birthday. Such treasured memories.

TIED IN NOTS

Damn, there must be something in this Rose Prairie air that's got me all in my feelings today.

Rosewood College campus sits sprawling before us as Jaxon pulls into the guest parking lot and cuts the engine. "What are we doing here?" I ask, as he shuts his door and jogs around to help me out of the car.

"Walk with me?" He holds his hand out and I gladly take it. Jaxon has worked wonders on my confidence, and he takes every opportunity that he can to show everyone that I am his. He raises our entwined hands to his mouth and kisses them.

He's turned oddly quiet as we walk past the old buildings we used to have classes in. We just pass the library when he pulls me to a stop. "Here, put this on." Reaching into his pocket, he pulls out a black handkerchief.

"Are you serious?" I laugh, while he covers my eyes with the fabric and secures it on my head with a gentle tug.

"Sure am." I can't see his smile, but I can hear it. I know that cocky grin I love so much is on his face and I want so badly to see it. Strong hands settle on my shoulders as he turns me quickly before grabbing my hand once more.

"What was that for? I can't see anything anyway."

"Well, Sweetness, I don't want you to know where we're going," he says matter-of-factly.

After several obstacle courses that I'm not sure were even there based on his laughs, the sound of trickling water reaches my ears as he pulls me to a stop. "Jax, I love you, but I hate to break it to you. I know exactly where we are."

His voice sounds off, stiff almost, as he responds. "I was counting on it. Sweetness, you can take off the blindfold now."

He doesn't have to tell me twice. This is my all-time favorite place in the entire world. The blindfold slides over my head and our bench sits before me, our initials carved into the armrest. "Hi, bench. I've missed you." Reaching down I pet the thing like it's a puppy.

"Sweetness?" Jaxon's voice comes from behind me, and I turn to see him kneeling on the pavement, ring box in hand.

My hands fly to my mouth in shock, my heart breaking out into a pounding pulse. I feel the heat of a blush spread across my skin as the love of my life patiently waits for me.

"Sweetness, three years ago I stumbled upon the greatest thing that's ever happened to me. It might have started out a bit rocky with a book to the face, but it's only gone uphill from there." He smiles nervously up at me as my tears drip off my cheeks. "This is our spot. This is where I first learned your name, where we found each other, and where I first told you I loved you. Now, Sweetness, I want this to be the place where you said yes. Will you marry me?"

Dropping to my knees in front of him, I throw myself at him. Ever steady, Jaxon catches me, clutching me close to him and I'm enveloped in his embrace. "Yes," I gasp, moving to bring our lips together.

It's official, *this* is my favorite place.

Thanks For Reading

Thank you for reading *Tied In Nots*.

When I started writing this story, all I knew was that it would be centered around a sweet, shy girl and her complete opposite sporty jock. The minute the name Candi popped into my head, my instant thought was, "No way in hell is her name going to be Candi." Of course, I was wrong.

The first day I started writing, the song Sugar, Sugar by the Archies played through my head, and it was a huge inspiration for this story. I can't tell you the number of times I listened to that song on repeat while writing this. So, thanks Mom for listening to oldies when I was growing up!

I hope you enjoyed being back in Rose Prairie and seeing all the things that Rosewood has to offer.

Be on the lookout for more Rose Prairie books!

If you could, please take a moment to rate and review on Amazon, Goodreads, Instagram, or wherever you post reviews. As an indie author, ratings and reviews are the best way of getting my work out there for other people to read. A little goes a long way!

Don't forget to follow me on Instagram @authorsierrashipley [1] and sign up for my newsletter[2] to get more details about my coming books!

---

1. https://instagram.com/authorsierrashipley?igshid=YmMyMTA2M2Y=

2. https://mailchi.mp/db7893726a2a/sierra-shipley-newsletter-sign-up-page

SIERRA SHIPLEY

Thank you for your support!
Until next time,
Sierra

You Don't Want To Miss This

See the Sneak Peek of
His Challenge[1]
The next book in The Claiming Her Series. Coming Soon.

Tanner

HAMMER AND STEIN CONSTRUCTION headquarters never fails to send shivers down my spine. The offices are full of people who don't work with their hands for a living like I do, prancing around the offices in suits and ties while I'm striding down the hall wearing steel-toe boots and dust-ridden jeans. It couldn't be helped. I was walking along the property where we will be breaking ground tomorrow when I got the call from the big boss.

Samuel Hammer, my boss, is the type of man that you don't fool around with. He's the 'rule with an iron fist' kind of boss. Thankfully, I've been working with him for several years now and we have an understanding of how the other works. He

---

1. *https://www.amazon.com/His-Challenge-Claiming-Sierra-Shipley-ebook/dp/*

   B0BMQJZ3DF/

   ref=sr_1_1?crid=2ZU482JAOTW8Z&keywords=His+Challenge+Sierra+Shiple

   y&qid=1675545701&sprefix=his+challenge+sierra+shipley%2Caps%2C128&sr

   =8-1

knows I will do my absolute best to run a safe and on-time job, which is how I earned the largest undertaking the company has had this year. In return, he will give me the space I need to complete the job without breathing down my back. Somehow, we make a good team.

Before the holiday season, the company put in a bid for a complete overhaul of a city block. That particular section of the city had basically been abandoned, full of empty lots with nothing going on. The city had reached out to every major construction company in the area for their project. We just happened to be the lucky bastards who were chosen.

In the once-empty lots, now bulldozed and leveled, will be a towering luxury condo, complete with upscale restaurants, coffee shops, and whatever else the upper elite deem worthy. Say what you want about Chicago, but the city is doing its damndest to try to revitalize it.

As I reach the conference room at the end of the hall, I attempt to straighten my t-shirt and open button-down shirt that is part of my everyday wear. As much as I don't like being down here, I'd also rather look a bit more put-together and professional, but what's a man to do? Letting out a deep breath, I gently tap on the door, letting those inside know I'm here.

The deep, rumbling voice of Samuel calls out, "Come on in, Tanner." Turning the handle, I step inside the long room, the wall of windows giving a view of the city beyond. Samuel is sitting at the head of the table, and the other upper management people in their tailored suits are sitting around the edges. It takes several long strides for me to reach Samuel, extending my rough hand toward him in a firm handshake.

"Mr. Hammer," I nod. I'm not entirely sure why I was called up here for an impromptu meeting, but I try to portray confidence as he gestures to an open seat. Clearing my throat, I sit, awkwardly glancing around the table. *What the hell is going on?*

The table grows silent as Samuel leans forward, settling his arms on the table. Sweat begins to break on the back of my neck, my unease breaking to the surface. "Now that everyone is here, Stein and I are announcing the expansion of Hammer and Stein Construction." The suits sitting around the table are all smiles, nodding their heads in excitement while I am just as confused as I've always been.

"This is a project we have been planning for several years and is somewhat of a passion project for me. I want Hammer and Stein to be the go-to Construction Company in Illinois, and that means expansion. It won't be ready for some time, but all of the people in this room are in the running for this business venture. Some of you, I know, are wondering what that means." He glances down each side of the long conference table, and I fight not to fidget under his gaze. "For some of you, like Mr. Williams here," he nods towards me, "means that a vertical movement up the ladder is a possibility, along with increasing salaries."

Is he saying he wants me to be one of the heads of the new branch? What the fuck? In the background, his droning turns into a low hum as I take in the weight of his announcement. This means that if I do my job above and beyond expectations, I will have a spot in upper management.

Holy shit.

As if I wasn't already nervous enough about this project, now I have a significant pay raise and promotion in the works. This could be a huge step for me. Sudden panic settles into my bones at the added pressure of this job. *I have to blow this whole thing out of the water.*

The meeting continues for thirty more minutes, none of which applies to me. So, what did my mind do with the added time? Played through every possible outcome of this project, running through the different scenarios and looking for ways to bypass any foreseeable problems.

Everything suddenly focuses when the sound of my name catches my attention. Snapping up, my head swivels around the table to identify who was trying to get my attention. It was my goddamn boss.

"Mr. Hammer?"

"I was saying how big of a deal this could be for you, Tanner. This project will determine where you head next. I'm looking forward to seeing the outcome of your work."

Standing, I work a gulp down my suddenly swollen throat. Offering my hand, I thank him before quickly leaving the building as fast as my feet could carry me.

About the Author

Sierra Shipley is a born and raised Midwest girl. She spends her days with her lovable rescue pup, Trip. Her ideal day is spent drinking coffee, reading, and dreaming.

Sierra has always wanted the romance she's read in books. Pair that with an active imagination and a love of creativity, and you get a writer!

Her goal is to create steamy, romantic stories with characters that people can relate to.

www.ingramcontent.com/pod-product-compliance
Lightning Source LLC
Chambersburg PA
CBHW030349180626
46812CB00007B/2819